JUST FOR THIS MOMENT

KAIT NOLAN

Just For This Moment

Written and published by Kait Nolan

Cover design by Lori Jackson

Copyright 2016 Kait Nolan

AUTHOR'S NOTE: The following is a work of fiction. All people, places, and events are purely products of the author's imagination. Any resemblance to actual people, places, or events is entirely coincidental.

To everyone who's ever felt like a black sheep,

This love story is for you.

With love,

Kait

Dear Reader,

This book is set in the Deep South. As such, it contains a great deal of colorful, colloquial, and occasionally grammatically incorrect language. This is a deliberate choice on my part as an author to most accurately represent the region where I have lived my entire life. This book also contains swearing and pre-marital sex between the lead couple, as those things are part of the realistic lives of characters of this generation, and of many of my readers.

If any of these things are not your cup of

tea, please consider that you may not be the right audience for this book. There are scores of other books out there that are written with you in mind. In fact, I've got a list of some of my favorite authors who write on the sweeter side on my website at https://kaitnolan.com/on-the-sweeter-side/

If you choose to stick with me, I hope you enjoy!

Happy reading!

Kait

"WELL? WHAT DO YOU think?" Myles Stewart sat across the table, trying to read the inscrutable face of his lunch companion.

Simone chased the bite of muffaletta with sweet tea and lifted her arm to get the attention of their waitress.

Corinne wandered over, more sass in the sway of her hips than she'd had when Myles moved to Wishful seven months before. He hadn't gotten the story on her yet. "Get you a refill on that tea, hon?"

"I'd like to speak to the cook."

"Something wrong with your sandwich?" Corinne asked.

"I'd just like to speak to the cook," Simone said evenly.

With a worried frown, the waitress headed back to the kitchen.

"What are you doing, Simone?"

She just lifted a sardonic brow and continued to sip her tea.

Myles glanced back to the kitchen where Mama Pearl Buckley, Goddess of Pie and Gossip and owner of Dinner Belles Diner, stepped through the door. Her brows drew down in thundercloud formation as she looked Simone's way.

Oh, this is not good. Not good at all.

"Seriously, if something's wrong, they'll fix it. There's no need to call Omar out."

"Omar, huh?"

Omar Buckley, master of the kitchen and Mama Pearl's youngest son, pushed into the room, a grease spattered apron stretched across abs that were just as flat as they'd been when he'd played on scholarship as running back for Ole Miss eight years ago—before the knee injury that blew his football career. Myles had heard that sad tale over coffee several months back. Omar's face was a twin of his mother's, and he had the shoulders and arms to back up his displeasure.

Shit. The last thing Myles needed was Simone making enemies her first day on the job. Myles could see the headline now. *Out-of-Towner Earns Buckley Wrath—Banned From Diner for Life.*

The lunch crowd went silent as Omar's shadow fell over the table. Everyone waited with bated breath to see how things would unfold.

"Somethin' I can do for you? Ma'am." This last he added after a pause.

Simone tipped her head back, blatantly scanning him from head to toe and back again, her lovely, mocha-colored face absolutely deadpan. "Omar, I presume?"

"Yeah."

"I just wanted to shake the hand of the man who made the best damned muffaletta I've had outside the French Quarter."

Myles released an audible breath.

The tension in Omar's face smoothed into a grin. "That a fact?"

"I lived there for close to ten years, so I'm in a position to know." She offered her hand. "Simone Grayson."

Omar took it, his bigger palm swallowing Simone's. "You visiting?"

"New in town. Glad to know I'll be able to satisfy at least some of my culinary cravings for N'Awlins."

Now that the threat was past, Omar made his own lazy survey of Simone, ending with an expression that said he'd be happy to satisfy any craving she had, culinary or otherwise. And Simone wasn't shutting him down. Wasn't that interesting?

As the silence stretched out between them, charging like a freaking Duracell, Myles fell back on old social training for proper introductions. "Simone's the new full-time reporter for *The Observer*."

"That right?"

"Omar does a bi-monthly food column for the paper. He rotates out with Tom Thatcher from The Spring House."

"I look forward to testing out some of your recipes."

"You do that. And if you have a hankering for somethin' in particular, you let me know. I might can do somethin' about it."

Simone smiled, and Myles was put in mind of a cat that'd cornered a particularly tasty form of prey. "I'll keep that in mind. Thanks."

As Omar headed back to the kitchen, Simone dove into her muffaletta in earnest.

"You need a cold shower?" Myles asked. "Because I'm pretty sure you just cranked up the temperature in here a good fifteen degrees."

She shrugged. "Let's just say I'm more than a

little glad I let you talk me away from *The Times-Picayune*."

"And I consider that one of my greatest coups. I told you you'd love it here."

His phone dinged, signaling a reminder. Myles slid it from his pocket and glanced at the screen. **Call Piper up for a date**.

Myles couldn't stop the grin from stretching ear to ear.

Finally.

He'd met Piper last September, during auditions for the Wishful Community Theater production of *White Christmas*. As Bob to her Betty, he'd held her, kissed her, spent hours with her on set and off. And he'd gone more than half crazy for her in the process. But the lovely and talented Piper Parish did not date her co-stars. Some B.S. about the false intimacy of the stage, which had seemed reasonable at the time he'd agreed to it. He'd been waiting three months. Months where they didn't get to hang out or talk more than the occasional text. Well, and the monthly karaoke night up at Speakeasy Pizzeria. The woman *loved* her karaoke and damned if he hadn't gone and learned half the music from Broadway just for the chance to sing with her. But that was more a group thing, not a one-on-one hang out opportunity. So he'd kept waiting. Ninety long, lonely days for her self-imposed edict to pass. And now, time was up.

Hot damn.

Maybe he could swing by the clinic where she worked to ask her in person before he headed back to the paper.

"You're looking awfully happy."

"Why wouldn't I be happy? I stole one of the most talented reporters I've ever had the pleasure of working with from one of the best papers in the country, I'm having a damned fine cheeseburger for lunch, and the paper is finally turning an actual profit."

"A good thing, too, as I'd like to actually get paid."

No sooner had Myles shoved the phone back into his pocket, then it beeped again, this time with an incoming text. He fished it out and read the message from his general Jill-of-All-Trades, Patty Hamilton, who he'd inherited when he bought *The Wishful Observer*.

Patty: **Your investor's attorney is here.**

Myles frowned.

"Something wrong?" Simone asked.

"Not sure." He texted Patty back. **Did we have a meeting scheduled?**

Patty: **No. He won't say what it's about.**

He? Not the usual woman?

Patty: **No. Never seen this one. According to his card, he's one of the partners from her firm in Atlanta.**

That was…odd and more than a little disconcerting. What could he want?

Be there as soon as I finish up lunch.

Looked like he wouldn't get the chance to swing by the clinic to see Piper after all.

Because he didn't want to wait, he thumbed

a quick text to Piper. **Time's up, Buttercup. When can I see you?**

Like some love-struck teenager, he stared at the phone, hoping to see the little gray bubble with dancing ellipses that would indicate an immediate reply. But there was nothing. And hell, the clinic could be under a rush with God knew what. They were smack dab in the middle of prime-time sinus infection season. She wasn't about to be texting when she was supposed to be taking blood pressure or temperatures or giving somebody a shot.

Calling himself an idiot, he put the phone away and finished inhaling his lunch. Simone got the rest of hers to go—which came complete with Omar's number scrawled on the Styrofoam box—and they hot-footed it across the town green and down the street to the humble offices of *The Wishful Observer*.

Myles didn't let himself get uptight or worried. His investor probably just wanted another progress report or additional explanation of some of the expansions Myles wanted to make. The hot-shot lawyer out of Atlanta was probably just stopping by because he was on his way to somewhere else.

Right, because Wishful is so on the beaten path?

By the time he stepped through the doors, Myles was willing to concede he felt a little bit nervous about the drop-in meeting. Those infantile nerves turned into awkward tweenagers at the sight of Patty's face.

"What?" he asked her.

"He's in the conference room. Just sitting there like an extra in a *Terminator* movie."

"Are we talking T-800 here or T-1000?"

"Tough call. I wasn't brave enough to try to kosh him over the head to see if he liquefied to fix himself."

Simone looked impressed. "You know *Terminator*?"

"Please. I have three sons. I don't know what he wants, Myles, but be careful in there."

Wanting to reassure her, he squeezed Patty's shoulder. "It'll be fine."

Stepping into the small conference room, Myles thought perhaps this guy should've auditioned as an extra for *The Matrix*. He looked like a better dressed Agent Smith, and Myles half expected to see an earwig partially covered by the perfectly cut brown hair.

"Mr. Stewart." When the words didn't come out with the same measured tone as Mr. Anderson, Myles was almost disappointed. This guy had a cultured, country club Southern drawl—the kind of accent Myles could imagine him practicing in front of a bathroom mirror, while quoting Atticus Finch.

"That would be me. I'm afraid you have me at a disadvantage, sir."

"I'm John Bondurant, from Bondurant, Meadows, and Leach. I'm here on behalf of your investor."

He didn't offer his hand to shake, so Myles dropped into a chair. "Of course. What can I do for you, Mr. Bondurant?"

"My client has reviewed the latest progress reports you forwarded on and is, quite frankly, disappointed in the profit and loss statements."

As unease slithered through him, Myles wished desperately they were in his office, where his desk was covered in toys he could pick up to occupy his hands. What he would give for a Slinky just now. "I realize the profit margin is a bit thin right now, but I've had less than a year to get the paper turned around. Some of the equipment needed updating, and I've had to expand my staff to accommodate the increased workload." If you could call moving from three employees to four and adding a high school intern a real staff expansion.

"Nevertheless, my client is concerned that your rather...ambitious plans are more optimistic than realistic."

"Change takes time. And businesses of any variety require solid investment before they really have an opportunity to grow." How many times had he heard that refrain growing up? Damn it, he knew business, and he knew newspapers. What he was doing here was working. Rome wasn't built in a friggin' day.

Mr. Bondurant pulled a folder from his shiny leather briefcase. "My function today is as messenger, Mr. Stewart. You needn't justify yourself to me."

Eying the folder like it would bite him, Myles slowly reached out and took it. There were only a few sheets inside. He pulled his reading glasses from his inside jacket pocket and read through the papers, feeling his cheeseburger congeal and harden with every word.

"This is insane. I can't possibly have the full payment on the loan by then. That's not even two months! This isn't what we agreed to."

"On the contrary, my client is exercising the right to pull out of the investment. In light of last quarter's returns, my client is well within rights according to the original agreement."

"Well, we need to revisit the damned agreement, then. This is ludicrous. I want to talk to your client. Directly."

"That's not possible. My client deals only

with proxies. I'd be happy to take your counter offer back and present it, but I advise you, Mr. Stewart, to begin looking for other investors. The loan payment is due at the end of the forty-five days or you forfeit ownership of the paper."

"THEY'LL MAKE such beautiful babies, with her pretty face. Better hope for a boy first because those girls will be so pretty, they'll need a big brother to beat the boys off."

Why did I let Mom and Leah talk me into this?

Piper Parish sat in the middle of a long table at the Wishful Country Club, as black-and-white clad wait staff wove around the bridal party, removing the salad plates—spinach and strawberry salad with poppyseed dressing, of course—contemplating whether it might be more enjoyable to stab herself in the eye with her salad fork, as she listened to her Great Aunt Beatrice extol the virtues of the bride-to-be. Carrie Jo was a jobless, twenty-two-year-old, barely out of college, who had no actual aspiration in life beyond getting her MRS degree, which she'd be achieving on Saturday. She was also Piper's cousin, which was exactly how Piper had been roped into being part of the bridal party. Considering she had actually changed Carrie Jo's diapers, that was a little bit demoralizing.

As the main course appeared—nothing but chicken salad would do for a bridesmaids' luncheon—Piper wondered if she could get away with ordering a mimosa or three in the name of celebration. Given this was the Southern Baptist side of the family, she thought not.

More's the pity.

"I heard Richard wants her to stay home so they can go ahead and start trying for a family."

Yeah, that's because they already got started on that part.

Not that Carrie Jo had mentioned it. But as a nurse, Piper was well-attuned to the signs. That glow sure as hell wasn't wedding happies. She wasn't showing yet, and Piper was reasonably sure no one else in the family knew or suspected. Considering the holy hell that would break loose if they found out—at least before Saturday—Piper wasn't about to be the one to reveal that secret. Let Carrie Jo have her day with as little drama as possible.

"So, when are we going to be hearing wedding bells for you, Piper?" Aunt Bea asked. "You've already let Leah beat you on that one."

Piper sipped at her sweet tea and muttered. "Last time I checked, marriage wasn't NASCAR." Not that anybody in her family recognized that fact. Her baby sister had beat her in the race to the altar three years prior, at the ripe young age of twenty-four. And she'd delighted the entire family by immediately providing the first grandchild a year later. A boy, Preston, who, Piper was forced to admit, was cute as the dickens. Leah was winning points left and right.

The remark earned her an aggravated look from her mother. It was an expression Piper was intimately familiar with.

"What's that, dear?" her great aunt asked.

"Nothing. No wedding bells for me any time soon, Aunt Bea."

"Oh, that's a shame. But surely there's someone special?"

Because the idea that her life could revolve around something other a man certainly didn't compute.

Before Piper could think of a snark-free reply to that, her phone vibrated. It was purely verboten that she had it out of her purse at all, but if she was caught, she had the excuse of being on-call at the clinic. Not that she actually was today, but they didn't know that.

She slid the phone from beneath her napkin and swiped to unlock the screen.

Myles: **Time's up, Buttercup. When can I see you?**

Piper's cheeks warmed, and she had to fight back the grin tugging at her lips.

Speaking of someone special.

The new-in-town and very sexy Myles Stewart had been her unexpected co-star in last fall's production of *White Christmas*. He'd been at auditions to write a story about the show and decided to audition himself just for the chance to meet her. She'd spent the last months of autumn fighting the zing between them, sticking to her self-imposed rule about not dating her romantic lead. He hadn't blinked when she'd issued a cool-down period so that whatever intimacy engendered by the show could fade. Instead, he'd spent the entire three months sending her outrageous texts and a daily notice of the countdown. She'd done her best not to respond too often, encourage him too much. But those texts had been the highlight of her days, keeping that zing alive and well and impatient. And then there was karaoke night. She lived for the chance to sing with him. They'd been carrying on the subtle flirtation through song all these months.

And now the wait was over.

Thank God.

Her thumb hovered over the screen, prepared to tap out a reply—*Is now too soon?*

"Piper!" The sound of her mother's voice almost made Piper drop the phone. "Are you on your phone?"

"No ma'am. I was just checking in with the clinic." Reluctantly, she slid the phone back into her purse beneath her mother's disapproving eye. She'd be hearing about this later.

Just as well she hadn't answered yet. Between work and all the wedding events, she wouldn't actually be free until after Saturday. Maybe Saturday night if the reception didn't run too late.

"What were you saying about who you were dating?" Aunt Bea asked.

Of course she hadn't lost that line of questioning.

Piper considered saying something about Myles, but the last thing she wanted was any of her nosy relatives going to bother him at work to find out who his people were. Besides, they weren't dating. Yet.

"I haven't had a lot of time for dating lately. We just recently wrapped the production of *The*

Mousetrap." She didn't usually go out for the non-musical roles, but she'd needed the distraction to keep from giving in to the temptation to blow her rule all to hell and jump straight into things with Myles—which, given the level of that zing, would likely have led straight to bed, thus breaking another personal rule. "Were you able to make it out to see the show? We got rave reviews."

"That's nice, honey, but you really should devote more time to finding yourself a husband. That biological clock is ticking and you don't have all that much time left."

"Right, because my ability to pop out babies is my only valuable attribute as a woman, and, at twenty-nine, I'm ancient and my uterus is populated by dust and cobwebs."

"Piper Elizabeth!" Her mother's middle name invocation brought all conversations at the table to a screeching halt. Nearly a dozen pairs of eyes fixed on her.

At Twyla's look of censure, Piper ducked her head. "Sorry, Mama."

This was her longest standing and most challenging role to date. Pretending to give a damn about what the rest of her family thought she ought to be doing with her life. Because certainly what she actually wanted didn't matter to any of them. God forbid she be anything but the traditional, dutiful, meek Southern daughter.

Carrie Jo's mama jumped into the conversational breach. "Piper, I'm just going over some last-minute details with the caterer," Jolene waved her own cell phone and nobody got on to her. "I think your reply card got lost in the mail. Do you have a plus one for the reception?"

This just keeps getting better and better.

She nearly said yes. For two long seconds, Piper considered asking Myles if he'd be her plus one. She doubted he'd say no and, God knew, his company would make the wedding less of a misery for her. But then her family would know about him. And he'd know about her family. Neither of those things seemed likely to lead to a desire for him to spend more time with her. Better to suck it up and admit the truth.

"No ma'am, I don't."

"Oh, that's a shame."

Piper called on all her acting chops to keep her smile fixed in place and set in polite rather than feral lines.

Carrie Jo's Aunt Rae spoke up. "I could set you up with Forest Langford. He's getting out again since his divorce."

"What about Quincy Blackmon?" Libby Newsom, the maid of honor, suggested.

Piper lifted a hand to stop the commentary and offers of pity dates. "No, really, it's all right. I avoided having a plus one on purpose."

They all stared at her as if she'd sprouted a second head.

"I just thought I could be of more help if I wasn't having to entertain a date. There's so much to manage, after all." A blatant lie, but it effectively turned the tide of pity.

"Well, isn't that just the sweetest thing?" Jolene declared. "Since you're…unencumbered, can I get you to—"

As Jolene took advantage of Piper's slip up to pile on additional wedding duties, all Piper could do was grin and bear it.

Three more days. Three more days and this insanity is over.

CHAPTER 2

"I'VE BEEN OVER THE contracts with a fine-toothed comb." Tucker McGee, attorney and sometimes community theater actor, sat back in his chair, an expression of regret on his face. "You're up shit creek, man."

Myles dropped his face into his hands. "I was afraid of that."

In the wake of Mr. Bondurant's departure, he'd flat out lied to his staff that everything was fine, then closeted himself in his office, working his ass off until day's end, and waiting until they'd all left to pull out the original contract to pore over it himself into the wee hours. He'd spent the last two days searching, in vain, for some other answer. Finding none, he'd brought them to his buddy to look over, hoping for some kind of miracle. No such luck.

"If you'd been my client when this whole deal went down, I'd never have let you sign this. Did you even read the whole thing?"

Myles bristled. "Yeah, I read it. But the possibility seemed so remote, it felt like it was worth the risk."

"Why?"

"I couldn't get a traditional bank loan large enough to fully buy out the paper. And the investor seemed perfectly happy to let me do my thing for the first year, once I explained my business plan. I never dreamed he'd want to pull out before the year was even up."

"That's the shitty thing about the law. It doesn't leave room for assumptions."

"But it makes no sense. He knows I can't buy him out. He's seen the quarterly reports. If he takes the paper in exchange, he's left with something he's already seeing as a poor investment."

"Which he could then turn around and sell," Tucker pointed out.

"Good luck with that. Do you know how long the paper sat on the market before I came along? Newspapers around the country are folding left and right. There aren't many people crazy enough to take it on. Probably fewer who could make it work. Selling isn't likely to make him back what he's put into it."

"You could counter with a new offer that gives the investor more oversight into the running of things. Feeling more in control of things might pacify him, if he's concerned about levels of profit and loss. If he agreed, it might get you a stay of execution."

Myles shoved up from the chair and began to pace around Tucker's office. "No. I'm not taking orders from some yahoo who knows nothing about the newspaper business."

"Well, at this point, you either come up with

the money to buy out the investor or forfeit controlling rights to the paper—which could put you in a position of being replaced entirely and having no say in things at all."

Hello rock. Meet hard place.

How the hell had he gotten himself into this mess?

That was a stupid question. He knew exactly how he'd gotten into this mess.

Veteran Newspaperman Forfeits Paper Due To Risky Investment.

He'd wanted to come home to Mississippi on his own terms, do his own thing, rather than finally joining the family business as had always been expected. He'd been so damned cocky about his odds of success turning *The Observer* around and dragging it into the twenty-first century, he'd agreed to less than favorable terms. And now if he didn't figure something out, he and his tiny staff would be paying the price.

The potential answer is staring you in the face, dumbass.

But that would mean taking Tucker fully into his confidence, something he hadn't done with anybody in Wishful since he'd moved here last September.

Is keeping that secret worth losing the business you've been killing yourself to build?

"There may possibly be a third option." Myles pulled another set of documents from his messenger bag. "Before he died, my grandfather set up a trust in my name. The terms are such that I've never had access to it up to this point, but my grandmother is executor. If I can convince her that this is a worthwhile cause, maybe she can override one of his stipulations."

Tucker took the copy of the trust and began reading through it. Other than a slight lift of brows, he showed no reaction to the contents. Myles made a note to remember that if he ever sat across from Tucker at a poker table.

"Well, that's one of the more unusual stipulations I've ever seen in a trust. Did he ever tell you why he tied this to you being married?"

"Apparently a man isn't truly settled down

and stable without a wife. I meet the rest of the criteria. I'm of age. Can my grandmother over-rule the marriage clause?"

Tucker shook his head. "She couldn't change that even if she wanted to. This thing is iron clad. It's marriage or nothing." He paused. "Although—"

"What?"

"There's no stipulation about divorce nulli-fying access once it's granted. Feel like a trip to Vegas?" Tucker grinned.

Myles snorted. "Some lunatic woman from a casino? Yeah, I can just imagine how my family would react if I brought someone like that home. I'm already the black sheep of the family. I'd just as soon not be completely disowned."

"Well, then, that leaves you with needing to find the money, either via other investors or fund-raising. I suggest you go talk to Norah about that. Hail Marys are kind of her specialty."

"No." Bringing in the city planner meant the whole thing likely became public knowledge.

Myles didn't so much care what the good citizens of Wishful thought about the financial situation of the paper, but he'd be damned if he'd give his father the satisfaction of knowing he'd been right. Warrick Stewart would delight in having the ammunition to take pot shots at Myles on every occasion.

"So, what are you going to do?"

"I don't know yet. But I've got forty-three days to figure it out." He took the contracts back from Tucker and shoved them into his bag. "Thanks for meeting with me on a Saturday to go over this. I'm sure you had better things to do."

"Yeah, the commute downstairs was a real bitch," Tucker joked. "You wanna come up for a beer? Watch the game? The Rebs are taking on Duke in about half an hour."

"Nah, my bracket's already busted." He wasn't in the mood for March Madness just now, even if his alma mater was doing well in the tournament.

"Offer stands if you change your mind."

Setting out from Tucker's office, Myles headed across the town green. He loved his adopted hometown. He loved living in a place where almost everyone knew his face, his name. Where he got a life story along with a cup of coffee. And where people still valued other people, putting them above the bottom line. He'd needed that change after years of anonymous living in cities across the country, slowly watching the evolution of journalism into the toy of corporate giants who'd forgotten that true journalism held people as its beating heart. No way was he about to give that up.

Myles hadn't realized he was heading for the fountain until he stopped in front of it. The heart of town, the huge marble fountain dated almost all the way back to the Civil War. Fed from nearby Hope Springs, it allegedly had the power to grant wishes. Norah's entire rural tourism campaign centered around the legend. Every light pole on Main Street flew the same banner: *Welcome to Wishful, Where Hope Springs Eternal.*

More apt to be cynical than not, Myles had to admit, the idea was appealing. Who couldn't use a little more hope in their lives? God knew he needed some just now.

Digging in his pocket, he pulled out a quarter.

Dear Universe, I wish for a way to save the newspaper.

With a flick of his thumb, he launched the coin into the air. It flipped, end over end, flashing faintly in the moonlight before it struck the surface of the water with a soft plunk.

Well, that's it then.

The phone in his pocket buzzed with an incoming text.

He pulled it out, grinning when he saw it was Piper. She was about the only thing that could make him smile right now.

Save me.

Myles thumbed a reply. **Where are you?**

Piper: **The Spring House for my cousin's**

wedding reception. They're Baptist, so no booze to numb the pain of boredom.

Myles: **That's tragic.**

Piper: **So are these bridesmaid dresses. Bile isn't exactly a flattering color.**

Myles: **You're kidding.**

Piper: **Wish I was. Shit. I've been made. Gotta go answer the call of duty. But after tonight, I'm free. See you soon!**

Shoving the phone back in his pocket, he changed directions and headed for his car. He might not know how to save the paper yet, but he could certainly save this damsel in distress.

Not bringing her own car was a serious mistake. Piper realized that just about the time the groom's handsy Uncle Eddie tried to get acquainted with her ass. For the second time. Despite the lack of alcohol being provided at the reception, he'd snuck in a flask and was sufficiently drunk that the sharp heel she jabbed "accidentally" into his foot didn't even make him flinch. One of Richard's brothers noticed and hauled Eddie off before Piper had to get more forceful.

She'd hoped, desperately, that the reception would wind down early and the bride and groom would do the whole bouquet toss and be eager to get on with the honeymoon. Instead, they seemed intent on dancing the night away in a last-ditch opportunity to party with all their closest friends. At least most of her duties as bridesmaid had been discharged. Short of post-reception clean up, she was free to enjoy herself. What a crock. Between dodging her relatives and friends of the family who seemed intent on asking every possible inappropriate question, from her relationship status to the state of her eggs—not in need of being cryogenically frozen, thank you very much—and trying to keep away from Uncle Eddie and others like him, she was bored out of her mind and desperate to escape. If the Spring House hadn't been a full ten miles from town proper, she'd have considered walking.

Ducking behind a ficus tree, she glanced around to make sure nobody was looking before tugging her phone out of the bodice of her dress. Not exactly the ideal place to carry it, but it wasn't as if these bilious monstrosities had pockets. Still no text back from Myles. Damn. She'd been hoping he'd entertain her a little.

Two strong hands slid over her hips from behind.

Before Piper could jam her elbow back into Eddie's gut, a voice whispered in her ear, "What's a pretty thing like you doing in a dress like this?"

Myles.

Her heart began to thud with excitement. "Does a line like that usually work for you?"

"Isn't that how it's supposed to work at wedding receptions? You come crash hoping to get a bridesmaid out of her dress?"

"You wouldn't have to work too hard to talk

me out of this one. But I demand pajamas as a replacement."

"That can be arranged." Myles pressed a kiss on the exposed skin of her nape.

Piper shivered and turned to face him, hating it when his hands fell away. "What are you doing here?"

"You asked for a rescue. I'm at your service, milady." He sketched a courtly bow, his mop of dark hair flopping into his eyes. Had he even had a cut since the show?

"Seriously?"

"I figured you were ready to get out of here. But if you want to make out in the coat closet, I'm good with that, too. I passed it on the way in. As I recall, you have a fondness for small, enclosed spaces."

"I did not drag you into that prop closet to make out," she reminded him.

"Such a waste. So how 'bout it? You want to make a break for it?"

She bit her lip, wondering if she'd even be

missed and calculating exactly how much hell she'd catch if she was.

"I've got a surprise for you back at my place," he coaxed.

"Is that a euphemism?"

His laughter skated over her skin. God she'd missed the sound of it these last three months. "Only if you want it to be. But I can promise you quiet and jammies and stove-top popcorn if you don't. Or we can go out, if you'd rather. But I figured you'd had enough of people tonight."

He was right. The whole scenario sounded like heaven.

"Let's get out of here."

After retrieving her purse, they snuck out via the veranda doors and circled around to where he'd parked his car. The cool air felt wonderful on her heated skin after the press of bodies inside. The moment she was buckled into the front seat, she slid her heels off and flexed her poor, abused toes. "God, that feels so good. I've been in these things since eleven this morning."

Myles shot her an incredulous look. "What time was the wedding?"

"Four. You guys have no idea how easy you have it. On the bride's side, there's all this pre-wedding stuff. Manis and pedis. Hair appointments. Last minute dress alterations because the bride put on unexpected weight. All the attendant freak out associated with that. Then pictures—but none of the joint pictures because it won't do for the bride and groom to see each other ahead of time. Then the waiting and the nerves and the bride puking. Calming her down. Getting some ginger ale and crackers in her. Checking on guests, locating the missing guest book. Locating the attendant who's supposed to make sure all the guests actually sign the guest book. It's been a...production. So much freaking drama. All the groom's side has to do is show up, put on a tux, and go."

"Jesus. I'll throw in a foot massage with the popcorn."

"You are a god among men, Myles Stewart." Piper dropped her head back against the seat.

"It's been mentioned once or twice. I'm guessing you are not one of those women into the big, fancy, invite-everyone-you-know kind of wedding?"

"I don't know why people don't just save the hassle and the expense and elope. Then have a big party for family and friends to celebrate when you get back. Seems simpler."

"Probably because various family members would be disappointed at the lack of pageantry."

She snorted. "Screw them. Marriage should be about the two people getting married and what they want. It's not about anyone else."

"Hear hear."

"Don't tell my mother. I've disappointed her enough by staying single until I'm nearly thirty."

"Oh, she and my grandmother can form a support group."

"I'm pretty sure that might be one of the most terrifying thoughts I've had in years."

"You're right," he said. "They'd be terrors together. New plan: Keep them as far apart as possible."

"Deal."

"I've missed the hell out of you, Piper."

"Back atcha." She smiled at him. "I nearly broke down and called you at least two dozen times."

He reached across the center console to tangle his fingers with hers. His expressive face was sober as he looked over. "Did anything change for you during that cooling off period?"

"Yes." He started to pull away, but she tightened her grip. "I got confirmation that this...thing between us has nothing to do with the roles we played on stage. Which is exactly what I wanted to know."

"Good. Because I'm just as crazy about you now as I was in December." His admission made her giddy. The kind of champagne bubble excitement she hadn't felt since she got her first kiss from Robert Hudson in *Meet Me in Saint Louis.*

She flexed her hand so she could trace a thumb around his palm. "I'm glad you waited around for me. A lot of guys wouldn't have."

"A lot of guys are dumbasses. Their loss."

They rode in comfortable silence back to his house. He pulled into the garage and put the door down. By the time she wedged her aching feet back into the heels, he'd skirted around the front of the car and opened her door. It felt just a little glamorous to take his hand and be helped out. Just a little reckless to be tugged up against his body, frissons of heat and awareness racing along her nerves.

He stepped back and let them into the house. "Now, let's get you out of that travesty of a dress."

Piper's pulse leapt with anticipation, but Myles didn't pull her into his arms. Instead, he released her hand and strode down the hall. Unsure what else to do, she followed. The bedroom was too minimalist to be his—no knickknacks scattered over the dresser or nightstand. She knew him well enough to know that he always had something readily available to occupy his hands.

He opened a bureau drawer. "What is it with women? It's like y'all save up every infraction against each other and unleash the revenge in the form of the most hideous possible bridesmaids dresses. What'd you do to your cousin?"

"Maybe it was that I enforced her bedtime one too many times when I babysat her as a kid."

"Well, if you want to have a ritual burning, it's not too warm for a fire." He handed over a set of pajamas.

Piper arched a brow. "I'm afraid the chemical fumes would kill us. This," she shook the dress, "just isn't natural. Should I be concerned that you just happen to have a set of women's pajamas?"

"My sister leaves some emergency stuff here for when she comes to visit."

"Well, there's something new. I didn't know you had a sister."

"And a brother, Grady. Both younger. Skye's the baby."

"Well, then I shall be grateful Skye's close to my size."

"Go on and get changed. I'll get started on the rest."

As he left the room, Piper wondered with pounding pulse just what the rest would be.

CHAPTER 3

MYLES HAD THE POPCORN on the stove and some of the kitchen chairs hauled into the middle of the living room floor by the time Piper came back out. He tried not to notice how the little tank top hugged her curves, but failed miserably. It wasn't that there was more skin exposed than there had been in the dress. It was the intimacy of seeing her in pjs. Didn't matter that he'd seen Skye in the same ones. He sure as hell hadn't been fantasizing about her for the last six months.

Piper crossed her arms, plumping up the breasts he was trying not to ogle.

"You want a sweatshirt or something? I didn't think about you getting cold." *Please say yes.* Myles had every intention of being a gentleman, but his will-power was only so strong.

"What on earth are you doing?"

"Huh? Oh." He lifted the edge of the comforter and finished draping it over the chairs. "I made you a blanket fort."

"A blanket fort?" The edge of confusion in her smile told him she didn't get it.

"You did tell me once that was your favorite scene in *The Holiday*. I thought it'd be fun to watch it with you from a blanket fort."

"That's—"

Stupid? Silly? Crazy?

"—awesome." She flashed him the smile that'd been haunting his dreams. "What can I do to help?"

"Go nab the rest of the pillows and comforter from the guest room."

He grabbed her one of his sweatshirts, while

she was at it, then went to check on the popcorn, which he barely saved from burning. By the time he'd dumped it all in a bowl and added salt, she'd also robbed the pillows from his room and some from the sofa and made a cozy little nest beneath the impromptu canopy in front of the TV. She'd also put on the sweatshirt —thank God.

He queued up the movie and crawled in to join her, loving that she immediately snuggled in. And then he could feel all those curves he was trying not to think about, despite the sweatshirt. But at least he had his arm around her. She balanced the popcorn on her lap, tossing some into her mouth as the title credits started.

"This was a fabulous idea," she said.

"I had at least a couple dozen different plans for our first date during the hiatus. Karaoke among them."

"Oh yeah?"

"But ultimately I decided I wanted you all to myself." Myles turned his head, taking advantage of the fact that her hair was still pinned up to press another tiny kiss to the sensitive skin behind her ear. Her shiver made him smile.

Piper turned her head, leveling those big brown eyes on his. "And what exactly are your plans for me, Mr. Stewart?"

"Something along the lines of making up for lost time," he murmured.

She was the one who tipped forward, closing the distance between them. Myles hummed low in his throat as she fitted her mouth to his, no hesitation, just a slow, easy exploration. There'd been no time for this with any of their stage kisses. He knew the heat that lingered just below the surface, just waiting to hit flashpoint. He'd felt it the night he'd kissed her the first time, outside Speakeasy. Had dreamed of it in the months since. But he didn't press. He'd follow whatever pace, whatever tone she set.

She shifted, twisting to better face him. Myles blindly set the popcorn aside, dimly grateful they hadn't gotten around to opening the Cokes as she wrapped her arms around him and took the kiss deeper. He slid his hand beneath the sweatshirt, feeling the heat of her skin through the thin tank beneath.

Just a little touch.

Snaking his hand beneath the tank, he spread his palm against the small of her back. Piper let out a sexy little moan and opened to him, her tongue darting out to dance with his.

For a moment, Myles thought his butt cheek had gone to sleep from sitting on the floor. Then he realized his phone was vibrating in his pocket. He growled in annoyance, wishing it to silence.

Piper broke the kiss. "Do you need to get that?"

"Right now, I don't care if the world is ending outside those doors. I've got good sturdy locks. They'll keep the zombies out."

"But what if it's something to do with the Sunday edition?"

He tucked a lock of hair that'd fallen free back behind her ear. "I both love and hate that you thought of that." Heaving a sigh, he wiggled until he could get his phone out of his back pocket. It'd stopped ringing, but the readout said the call was from Simone. "Crap. I should probably call her back."

Piper sat back, straightening her sweatshirt and grabbing the bowl of popcorn.

"Just don't—I'll make this quick."

Her feline smile made his blood heat. "I'm not going anywhere."

Myles crawled out of the blanket fort because there was no way he'd be able to concentrate with the temptation of Piper right there. "You want anything while I'm up?"

"Napkins. The popcorn is a little greasy, as all good popcorn should be."

"You got it." He hit the call button as he headed to the kitchen.

Simone answered on the first ring. "Bad time?"

"Kind of. Is this important?"

"Uh oh. That's your you-better-not-cock-block-me voice."

"I do not have a tone for that."

She laughed. "Don't be lyin'. I knew you straight out of college."

"I cannot be held accountable for my actions in the French Quarter at twenty-four. What do you need?"

"There was a development in the front page story for tomorrow. I wanted to go over the proposed changes. I'll be quick."

"Go then."

He passed Piper some paper towels and switched on his editor mode. Simone was right. The whole conversation took less than ten minutes. He made his decisions and gave her last minute instructions for putting the paper to bed. Cameron Diaz's character had just arrived at Rose Hill Cottage by the time he hung up. But for just a moment, he stood there, trying to switch the inner newspaperman back off. Because talking to Simone had brought the whole goddamned mess with his investor back to the forefront of his brain.

"Myles?" Piper had crawled out of the blanket fort. "Everything okay?"

He tossed the phone onto the end table and forced a smile. "Yeah, everything's fine." Crossing to her, he laced his hands behind her back. "Now, where were we?"

She stopped his mouth with two fingers. "You forget, I've seen you act. Seriously, what's wrong?"

Myles hesitated.

"I mean, you're free to tell me it's none of my business, but when people I care about are upset, I like to try to help."

He loved that instant support, loved, too, the idea that he was someone she cared about. But did he really want to drag her into all of this? "It's not that. It's just—Hell. I'm not gonna be able to turn it off. Let's go back to the fort for this story."

"All things are better in a blanket fort," she agreed.

He paused the movie and they set up on opposite sides this time, each leaning against a chair. Myles picked up one of her feet and began the foot rub he'd promised. "So, you know I'm editor of the paper. What you may not know—what very few people know—is that I also own it."

Her eyes widened. "Seriously? Aren't newspapers usually owned by big conglomerates or whatever?" Her question trailed off on a moan as he dragged a knuckle down the arch of her foot. The sound almost derailed his brain entirely.

What was he saying? *Oh, right.*

"Often. Small-town ones less so. When I left Philadelphia, I wanted to take a struggling small town paper and turn it around. I wanted my stamp on it. My vision. The only way to ensure I was able to do that was to buy it outright."

"That must have been crazy expensive."

"It was. I couldn't get a traditional loan to do it, and I didn't have enough capital of my own. So, I had to take on an investor."

She was an attentive audience, listening

without interruption, as he spilled out the whole sorry tale.

"Basically, I'm out of options, unless I take Tucker's suggestion and hit up Vegas."

Amusement lit her eyes at that idea. "Well, you could go find yourself a showgirl on the strip. Or you could take the more obvious answer."

"Which is?"

"Marry me."

MYLES' face went slack with shock. "Are you drunk?"

Piper didn't take offense at the question. "Sober as a judge. Baptist wedding, remember? Just hear me out. If you show up with some total stranger in tow that you picked up in Vegas or wherever, your grandmother will, I presume, flip her lid."

He grimaced. "That's putting it mildly."

"As executor of the trust, might she have the

option to *still* not give it to you if she thinks you got married strictly for the money?"

"I'd have to check with Tucker to verify, but maybe," he said slowly.

"Whereas if you come with me, it's more believable. We have backstory because of the show. As far as they know, we fell for each other on stage, started dating. Six months is quick but not insane crazy short for getting engaged."

Myles stared at her. "But I have to be actually *married.* Legally. License and all."

"We do a quick courthouse ceremony somewhere out of town. We have all the legal stuff in place for you to take to your family. Nobody here has to know, and we can just continue on dating as if nothing has changed." She paused. "Assuming you still want to date."

"So, you're suggesting we get married and then date?"

"Basically. The terms of the trust are satisfied, you get the money to pay off your investor, and everybody gets to keep their job."

She could see his nimble brain sorting through scenarios, trying to find all the angles. Her own mind hummed, bouncing like a prize fighter just waiting to knock down the next question or objection. They could really do this and he'd be able to save his business.

"Where would you live?"

"As far as anyone here would be concerned, we'd just be dating, so I'll keep my place."

"What about holidays? Thanksgiving. Christmas. Your family will expect you there. And mine will think it's weird if you don't show up with me."

"Your family's in Madison, right? It's less than two hours away. I'm sure we could juggle it. Work is always a convenient excuse to need to change the time of something. We could make this work, Myles."

"Okay, say I consider this—and that's a big if, because this may be the most madcap scheme I've ever heard—how long would we keep this up?"

"Long enough for you to gain access to the trust and…" Piper hesitated.

"And what?"

Nothing risked, nothing gained. This wasn't any crazier than the rest of what she was suggesting. "And long enough for us to figure out whether we want it to be a permanent thing or not."

"Permanent?"

For all that she'd learned to read his expressions when they'd worked together on stage, she couldn't read him now. Had *that* been the point to scare him away from her? Pretending a casualness she didn't feel, she kept her voice light. "That's kind of the point of dating, isn't it? Deciding whether you want a permanent relationship or not. We'd still be doing that, albeit unconventionally."

"Fair point. And if it doesn't work out?"

She shrugged. "Then we get a quiet divorce, no harm, no foul. Tucker told you there was no contingency in the trust to take the money away if you did. And I'll sign a prenup relinquishing whatever rights I might hold over it as your wife."

He scrubbed both hands over his face and back through his hair, making it stand up in the back. "You realize this is completely insane, right? You're suggesting actual, legal marriage with the same casual attitude you might take to leasing a car."

"I trust you. I wouldn't be here with you now, wouldn't have made this offer, if I didn't. I'm suggesting that you actually like me. You—I presume—trust me. You know I can act, so I can sell whatever needs selling to your family to legitimize things. If nothing else, we're friends, with an obvious potential to be more. I have no other encumbrances to keep me from helping you out with this, and it'll either end as quietly as it begins or..." Piper didn't want to give too much thought to exactly how much she wanted to believe in that "or".

"Or we decide to stay married. What then? Do we just come out and tell your family and our friends about this lunacy?"

Stay married. Wouldn't that be something? To jump into this with the intent of helping a friend and find forever. It wasn't why she'd offered, wasn't what she expected. But if that was how it played out? She'd consider herself lucky that the gamble payed higher dividends than she'd counted on.

"Either that or we elope somewhere far away where nobody's liable to show up. We could have a second ceremony as a vow renewal or skip it and take a honeymoon. Nobody's likely to question it."

"Speaking of honeymoon…" He trailed off, obviously looking for a polite way to phrase what he wanted to say.

"To be clear, I'm not talking about marriage in name only, if that's what you're wondering. I think it's pretty obvious I'm attracted to you. If we do this, we *are* married, and I expect exclusivity and all the—shall we say, benefits—that go with it."

His expression shifted to one of such

hunger, Piper began to wonder if she could get an advance on those benefits.

"One way or the other, I'm not interested in being with anyone but you."

"Same goes," she agreed.

They stared at each other, her waiting, him apparently out of questions.

"And I thought the setup you pulled on Tyler and Brody was nuts." Myles shook his head.

Piper shrugged with more nonchalance than she felt. "It was just a suggestion."

"What if someone here finds out?"

"Which part?" Was he embarrassed about the idea of being married to her?

"The whole secretly married and not actually living together part. That brings up all kinds of questions and awkwardness. I don't want to make things weird for you with your family."

She snorted. "Sweetie, things are permanently weird for me with my family. The idea that I had a husband would be the first thing I'd ever done they thought was right or proper, no matter how it came about. I am the ultimate black sheep there, so don't let that deter you. And either way, I don't see how they'd find out. You've said yourself your family never comes here. Well, except apparently your sister, and it'd be easy enough to stay over when she does."

Myles stared. "You've got it all figured out, don't you?"

"It's just not that complicated."

"Not that—Your mind works in devious ways, Piper Parish. It's one of the things that fascinates me."

"I'm not afraid of risk. You already know that about me, so none of this should come as a surprise to you."

"Oh, I have a feeling you'll still be surprising me in fifty years." He scrambled up. "Be right back."

Future tense. Not just the possibility of it. He was going to bite.

Oh boy.

Because her throat was dry, Piper popped

the top on her Coke and took a long swallow. He was right. This was completely nuts. She'd just proposed what was essentially a marriage of convenience. It was well-intentioned, of course. But like all of her crazy schemes, it had the potential to backfire. Did she really want to go through with this?

What's the worst that could happen? We get divorced and I lose his friendship. I'd hate it, but I got along just fine without him before. I could do it again. Isn't it worth the risk to help him save his business and the jobs of everyone who works for him? And what if it turns out to be the real deal?

Myles crawled back inside the blanket fort, this time settling beside her. "Give me your hand," he ordered.

She gave it without hesitation.

"You are, without a doubt, the single most interesting woman I've ever met. You're funny, smart, gorgeous, and you've got the biggest heart of anyone I know. If you're truly serious about this, I'd be honored if you'd be my partner in crime and marry me." He held out a ring in his other hand. The diamond glinted in the glow from the TV behind him.

Piper's mouth fell open. "You have *a ring?*" Her gaze shot back up to his. "Wait, why do you have a ring? Is there some failed engagement in your past I need to know about?"

He huffed a laugh. "No. Never got anywhere close to engaged before. It was my grandmother's," he explained. "Granddad got her a new set for their fiftieth anniversary and this came to me to pass on to the woman I want to marry. If I'm going to do this, I'm going to do it right. So, how 'bout it? You really want to go through with this?"

To actually marry this thoughtful, considerate, wickedly funny man in less than a month? "I really do."

"Okay then." He slid the ring onto her finger, then lifted her hand to his lips. "I'll do everything in my power to make sure you won't regret it."

No matter what happened, Piper didn't think she could possibly regret deciding to be with him. The weight of the band gave the whole situation an air of gravity she hadn't expected. They both stared at it on her hand for several long moments.

"So. Really engaged," she said, desperate to lighten the mood.

"Looks like."

"Well, I definitely didn't expect *that* when I left the house this morning. I didn't even catch my cousin's bouquet."

"Second thoughts already?" His tone was wry and joking, but there was something else beneath it. Regret? A sense that this whole scenario was too good to be true?

"No." Realizing she'd sounded less than convincing, she took his hand, waiting until he looked her in the eye to repeat it more firmly. "No."

"If you change your mind, I'll understand. It's a pretty snap decision."

Piper shook her head. "All of the best decisions in my life have been snap decisions. I'm good with this."

His eyes searched her face. Evidently, he saw whatever he needed to see because he relaxed and leaned back, tucking her into his side. "Okay then. Let's finish our movie."

Did he honestly think she'd be able to focus on a movie *now?* "Don't we kind of have a lot of details to figure out?"

"Yeah, but they can wait for tomorrow. The countdown will begin soon enough. Tonight, let's just get used to the idea that we're about to jump into the deep end of the pool."

Settling against him and tucking her head against his shoulder, she said, "Okay." *As long as you're with me to help tread water.*

CHAPTER 4

"ARE YOU SURE THEY shouldn't at least *meet* me first?"

From the driver's seat, Myles glanced over at Piper. "Why on Earth would I subject you to my family before the wedding?"

"Apart from the fact that it's kinda the way things are done?"

"Since when do you care about tradition on that front?"

"Okay, fair point. But it would add to the legitimacy. If we just show up married, they're bound to be suspicious. Whereas, if they've met me, gotten a chance to see that we're besotted with each other and know we're planning to get married, we can play off the elopement as a grand, spontaneous adventure and it'll be less of a surprise."

"Besotted?" He shot a glance at her, not sure whether he was offended by the term or not.

"What do *you* call spending every waking minute we're not at work either together or on the phone or texting?"

"Strategic planning?" he suggested.

She arched one perfect brow and pursed those kissable lips. "Strategic planning does not involve copious fondling of my ass."

"Well it should. It's a very fine ass."

"So's yours, as it happens. And yes, *some* of this last week has been planning and filling in the gaps in our knowledge about each other. But mostly we've been making up for that lost time in spectacular fashion. And loving every minute of it. Admit it."

"You got me there."

Piper grinned at him. "If the shoe fits,

sweetheart." She leaned across the center console to lay a smacking kiss on his cheek.

Her easy affection helped ease something in his chest. Since their engagement—Jesus, he still couldn't quite wrap his head around that—Myles had worried some that she saw this whole thing as a giant, long-running role. But during the show, he'd learned the difference between when she was acting and when she was being herself. This vivacious, relaxed woman had really hitched her metaphoric wagon to his. He'd been splitting his time between enjoying the hell out of the ride and worrying it would blow up in their faces any minute.

"Fine, I'll concede besotted. But I'm not bending on the rest. Not only because I don't want any of the blowback to hit you, but also because my family *is* one of the ones that does tradition and all that pomp and circumstance you dislike about weddings. If they get wind of it, my grandmother and mom will take over everything."

"There's this little two letter word. You might've heard of it. No."

"You don't know my grandmother. She's a force of nature. It's just simpler all around if we stick to the plan." He pulled the car into the Wachoxee County Courthouse parking lot. "Okay, if you're having second thoughts, now's the time to back out."

"I'm all in," she said, without hesitation.

"You're not nervous at all, are you?"

"No. Although we probably should've brought separate cars."

"Why?"

"What if we run into people we know?"

"We're forty-five minutes from Wishful. Who are we going to run into?"

"Need I remind you that Mississippi is one big small town? You never know."

"You're more likely than I am, and you've got those big movie star sunglasses blocking half your face and that scarf around your hair. It's very Audrey Hepburn."

She tipped those sunglasses down and

peered over the top of them. "You should've worn a hat or something."

"We'll be in and out in a matter of minutes. It'll be fine." He slid a hand around her nape and tugged her closer, reveling in how readily she leaned into the kiss. Once Piper Parish made up her mind about something, she didn't waffle.

"Mmm," she purred. "Let's go get a marriage license."

The circuit clerk's office was on the second floor, next door to the tax assessor's office. Being mid-morning on a Tuesday, there wasn't a line.

As they stepped inside, the clerk, a heavy-set, middle-aged woman beamed from behind the counter. "Can I help you?"

A public employee who actually likes their job. What a concept.

"Yes ma'am, we'd like to apply for a marriage license," he said.

"Certainly. Here's the application." She passed a clipboard across the counter. "And I'll need both your driver's licenses."

They handed the IDs over and took the clipboard over to a couple of vinyl covered chairs in the corner.

"You want to write or shall I?"

"My handwriting is probably neater," Piper pointed out.

Myles handed the clipboard over.

"Full legal name."

"Myles Beauregard Stewart."

"Beauregard? Really?"

"I cannot be held accountable for my parents' taste. What about you?"

"Piper Elizabeth."

"Your initials are PEP?" He grinned. "Were you a cheerleader in high school?"

"I was not. Show choir. And now you know why I do not fall prey to the Southern addiction to monogramming."

She filled in both their addresses, then paused. "Your parents' names and address."

"My parents? Why the hell do they need to know our parents' information? I'm over thirty for God's sake."

"It's probably to make sure we're not cousins or something."

Myles gave the information and watched her fill in her own.

"Mom's maiden name?" she asked.

"Myles."

"Ah, you're one of those, huh?"

"First born. It's a thing. I consider myself the lucky one. Also on the table was Clifton. I mean, really. Clifton Stewart?"

"I take your point. Highest grade completed in school? Bachelors or Masters?"

"Masters from Columbia."

"Columbia, huh? And how did you enjoy The Big Apple?"

"I missed the hell out of Southern cooking. Great night life, though," he admitted. "Anything else?"

"Am I correct in assuming there's no previous marriages hanging out in your closet that you've failed to mention?"

"Nope."

"Me either. Okay, we're done." Piper crossed to the counter and handed the application over.

"I'll just go get this typed up. You wait right there. Oh, and the fee is fifty dollars. Cash only."

Piper turned back to him. "Uh oh. Did you bring cash?"

"Got it covered. Come sit with me, future Mrs. Stewart. Although, under the circumstances, I guess you're not changing your name, are you?"

"I hadn't thought about it yet." She sat, lacing her fingers through his. "But yeah, under the circumstances, I guess it doesn't make sense."

"If things were different, would you want to? Take my name, I mean." He didn't know why it mattered, really. He understood all the reasons a woman might not want to take her husband's name, but a part of him was still old-fashioned enough to wish she'd at least want to, even if it wasn't practical.

"I'm not attached to my maiden name, and I

always figured I'd end up taking my husband's name when I married just as part of that whole forging a unit thing—unless it sounded ridiculous with Piper or was something heinous. There's this one girl I went to high school with who's now Amber Hopper Butts. I am pretty positive I can't love anybody enough to take the last name Butts."

Myles laughed. "Don't blame you there."

"But yes, if things were different, I'd take your name."

He lifted the hand he held to his lips. "Is it crazy that this is starting to feel less crazy? I keep waiting for reality to kick in, but all I can think about is you." How was it that in so little time together, she'd so thoroughly worked her way under his skin, into the very fabric of his life?

She shifted her hand to cup his cheek, staring into his eyes in a rare moment of seriousness. "Nothing great is ever gained without risk. You're worth the risk."

Had anyone ever believed in him that much?

Certainly not his family. He had no idea what he'd done to deserve her faith.

"Piper, I—"

"Here we go," said the clerk.

They crossed to the counter, still holding hands.

"I just need to get your signatures. You here, Mr. Stewart."

Myles signed where she indicated and passed the pen to Piper.

"And you just there, Ms. Parish."

Squeezing his hand, she scrawled her name.

The clerk, whose name plate read Dotty, took the cash and did whatever recording needed doing before handing the license over in an envelope. "You're all set. When's the happy day?"

"Oh, we haven't quiet set the date yet." Piper grinned. "We're eloping."

Dotty beamed. "Congratulations and best of luck to both of you."

They thanked her and stepped out into the hall.

"Well, that feels all official," he said.

"Are you having second thoughts?" she asked, one brow lifted.

Myles tucked her hand in his arm and smiled. "Not a one."

He made it all of two steps before someone stepped out of the tax assessor's office into their path.

"Oh, excuse me," the woman said, turning toward them.

"That's quite al—" He trailed off as recognition hit him. *Oh, please don't—*

"Why, Myles Stewart! I'd heard you were back in Mississippi after all these years. How's your grandmother doing?"

"She's just fine, Mrs. Healy." *Escape, escape. Must escape.*

"I saw that feature *Mississippi Magazine* did on her gardens. They're as lovely as ever."

"Yes ma'am." Myles wracked his brain for some kind of polite exit strategy before she started asking more questions.

The older women turned inquisitive eyes on Piper. "And who's this lovely young thing?"

Too late.

Before he could think of a reply, Piper offered her hand with a friendly smile. "Piper Parish. It's lovely to meet you Mrs. Healy. I'm so sorry to meet and dash, but I'm late getting back to work and Myles is being kind enough to drop me off."

She towed him, politely but firmly, down the hall, even as he called back, "Good to see you, Mrs. Healy. My best to Mr. Healy."

Neither of them spoke again until they were in the car.

"'It'll be fine,' you said. 'Who will we run into?' you said." Piper shot a glance back toward the courthouse. "Is that going to be a problem?"

"No. They were friends of my grandparents forever ago. They moved from Madison around the time I left for college, and I don't think she and my grandmother have been in touch since."

"And yet she'd heard you were back in Mississippi."

"That's probably because of the feature article about it in *Something Southern*."

"*Something Southern* did an article on you?"

"Despite my black sheep status in my own family, the rest of society seems to think I'm an eligible bachelor."

"Were," she corrected.

He liked the possessive gleam in her eye. "Were, indeed. Let's get you back to work."

"That's the eighth victim of this particular brand of cold in the last two days. I think we'd better get ready for a streak." Dr. Miranda Campbell scooped a hand through her thick blonde hair.

"Stock up on Kleenex and antibacterial wipes. Check." Shelby Abbott, the clinic office manager, scribbled a note on her ever-present list.

"How are we on the peroxide wipes and spray?" Piper asked, repressing a smile at the incoming text from Myles: **Prepping for staff meeting. Nerf dart gun or koosh balls?**

Never a dull day around The Observer.

"Low."

"Might want to add those, too," Piper suggested, rather wishing they had time for horseplay at their own staff meetings. "We haven't had a stomach bug in a couple of months. That always makes me nervous. It's coming."

"Fair point," Shelby conceded.

"Anything else I need to know about?" Miranda asked this with a pointed glance at Piper.

"What?" Piper asked, slipping the phone back into her pocket without answering the text.

"Just wondering when you're going to tell us who this mystery guy is you've been texting like a teenager. I'm working too much to date, so I'm living vicariously through you."

"How do you know it's a guy I'm texting?" she asked, all innocence.

"Because you've had that same secret, flirty

smile since high school," Miranda said. She crossed her arms. "Spill it, Parish."

Piper huffed a sigh, but couldn't seem to tame said flirty smile. "Myles Stewart."

"The guy who played Bob in *White Christmas*?" Shelby asked.

"The newspaper editor?" Miranda put in.

"Right on both accounts." Piper couldn't help the immediate aren't-I-a-lucky-girl blush.

"Totally not surprised," Shelby announced. "You two were shooting off sparks at that karaoke fundraiser. Everybody else was paying attention to Tyler and Brody, but I saw you." She smirked and tapped two fingers beside the eagle eyes that tended to miss nothing.

"How is it we didn't know about this?" asked Keisha Williams, one of the other nurses, as she handed Miranda a patient file.

"We've been keeping it quiet," Piper said, deliberately not mentioning how long they'd been seeing each other.

"Surprised he didn't have to beat them off

with a stick after that write up in *Something Southern*," Keisha said.

Piper had a sudden, entirely irrational desire to show off the engagement ring that nobody could know about. She had it on a very long chain around her neck. "Wait, you saw the article? *I* haven't seen the article. What was in this thing?"

"Mmm, best I recall, an account of his newspaper career to date and his plans for *The Observer*. Pics of the hottie in his element and all that. He's got a hella great smile."

"Yes, yes, he does," Piper agreed, unable to stop her own grin from spreading.

"Well, good for you," Miranda murmured absently, reading the file. "At least one of us has the good sense to have a life outside this place. I'm pretty sure I'm going to be buried here."

"Speaking of which, can I get off a week from Friday?" Piper winced, knowing she'd just asked off several days for Carrie Jo's wedding and half a day so she and Myles could go to Lawley yesterday.

"Check with the Schedule Master," Miranda told her. "I apparently have a broken finger to set in Room Three."

"Shelby?" Piper asked hopefully.

"I need to see if Noelle can come in to sub for you," Shelby replied. "If this cold epidemic escalates like we expect, we'll need someone else here."

"Okay, just let me know." Piper's phone buzzed in the pocket of her scrubs.

"Is that Myles?" Shelby asked in a sing-song voice.

Piper lost her smile as she read the message. "It's my mother."

Come home immediately.

Automatically, she called her mom's number. "Piper—"

Piper's stomach dropped. "Mom, what's wrong?"

"You need to come to the house, right now. It's an emergency." Her mother's voice sounded strained.

"What is wrong?" Piper demanded. "Is it Dad? Is he hurt? Is it—"

"Your father is fine. Nobody's bleeding or injured. Just come. Now."

Piper stared at her phone as the line went dead. "What the hell? She says it's some kind of emergency."

"We're not too covered up just now. Go. Let us know if we can do anything." Shelby waved her on.

Piper grabbed her purse and bolted for the door. Her brain switched gears, flipping through her mental Roladex of family members and their health conditions as she drove, wondering if someone had had a heart attack or, worse, died. Was it a relative? Had the cat finally given up the ghost? Was she about to be asking off for a funeral? Had Dad lost his job? What the hell else constituted an emergency big enough that she'd be pulled away from the clinic in the middle of the work day?

A shiny white Lexus sat at the curb in front

of her parents' house. Not a vehicle Piper recognized.

Okay, not a cop car, so probably no accident anywhere.

She let herself in through the kitchen door, immediately noting the scent of coffee and the fact that the good china was out. Who merited that kind of treatment? And what kind of emergency would prompt her mom to pull out the china? Or had the emergency happened after?

"Piper! Is that you?"

"Yes ma'am," she called. She could hear her mother's voice speaking to someone else as she hurried down the hall.

"...can clear this right up."

Clear what up?

Piper stepped into the living room, automatically assessing the situation for medical needs, despite her mother's assurance on the phone that no one was bleeding or injured. Her father turned from the empty fireplace, his expression strangely flat. Her mom perched on the edge of one of the Queen Anne chairs, a half-full cup of coffee clutched in nervous hands. The sofa was occupied by a beautiful woman with perfectly coiffed white hair. Her deep purple suit was clearly tailored and expensive, made of excellent fabric. Piper recognized the sedate pumps on her crossed ankles as designer. Though the woman's face had a few lines, it was impossible to tell whether she was sixty or eighty. She had that kind of gorgeous skin that spoke of years of disciplined care and privilege.

"Mom? What's going on? Where's the emergency?"

"This is our daughter, Piper," Her mother offered.

The older woman set down her own cup and folded her manicured hands, piercing blue eyes fixed on Piper. "I'm Suzanne Stewart. I understand you're marrying my grandson."

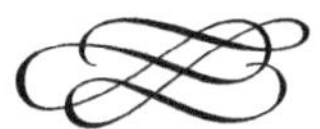

CHAPTER 5

"STATUS OF AD SPACE for Thursday's edition. Go." Myles hurled the Koosh ball at Wes Collier's head.

Wes snagged it out of the air with the practiced ease of a seasoned short stop, which was the position he played in the local softball league. "We've still got a half page open on page two, a couple of eighths available toward the middle and a quarter page ad empty in the sports section."

Myles' phone vibrated and his fingers itched

to pick it up, but he kept his attention focused on his staff.

"Hit up Adele Daly to see if she wants to run any kind of specials for The Mudcat in honor of March Madness for the sports opening," Myles ordered. "The weather's warming up, so the Co-op may have some kind of sale going on with spring plantings. Call Abe Costello to check on that. Cam Crawford at the nursery, too. And Speakeasy might want to announce the weekend's specials."

The phone vibrated again. Then again, dancing across the conference table, as what was apparently several texts hit at once.

"Maybe you should get that," Patty suggested.

Myles turned the phone over and swiped it open to see what was going on. The bottom dropped out of his stomach as he read Piper's messages.

I don't care what you're doing right now, drop it.

I need you.

This is a serious emergency.

Oh God, had she been in an accident? Before he could text back or call, another message hit.

Your grandmother is sitting in my parents' living room.

"Oh my God."

"Everything all right?" Patty's teasing expression shifted to one of concern.

"No. No everything is definitely not all right. Meeting adjourned. I...I have to go."

"But what about—" Zach began.

"Simone will decide. You're editor for the rest of the day. Whatever you say goes." He shoved away from the table, bolting for his office and his keys. By the time he hit the front door, he was running.

What the hell was Gram doing here? How did she even know? As he slammed the door and started the car, he remembered their brief encounter with Mrs. Healy.

Shit. Of *course* she used running into him as an excuse to call up Gram and catch up. But how had Gram found Piper's parents? Or their address?

The marriage license.

It wasn't filed yet, but they were public records. If she'd called the circuit clerk's office...

A litany of profanity and self-recriminations ping ponged through his head, cranking up in intensity as he screeched to a stop behind his grandmother's Lexus.

They'd been watching for him. The front door opened as he hurried up the walk. Piper stood in the doorway, face drawn and pale but for two flags of color in her cheeks. Her scrubs said she'd been called from work. Behind her, he could hear raised voices.

Myles ran the rest of the way, reaching for her instinctively, wanting to put himself between her and whatever was on the other side of that door. He cupped her jaw, feeling the tension. "Are you all right?"

She leaned into his touch. "It's nothing a stiff drink won't fix. Which would be expedient since I've all but been ordered to pee on a stick."

Absolute blistering fury ripped through him. Grabbing her hand, he pushed past her into the room. "Everybody quiet!" he bellowed.

All three of them shut up. Piper's parents looked shocked. The only change in Gram's expression was a faint lifting of those patrician brows.

Myles had to pause for several moments to rein in his temper enough to speak to her. "How dare you." He sucked in another breath that did little to calm him. "How dare you show up here, without my knowledge, certainly without my consent, and interject yourself to *interrogate* my fiancée."

Gram had the grace to look at least mildly regretful. "You know it had to be asked."

"No, it goddamned well did not."

She made a face at his language. "But your brother—"

"I am *not* Grady. And Piper sure as hell isn't some gold-digging trollop who'd try to pass someone else's baby off as mine. And not that it's *any* of your business, but there is no possibility of a baby because we haven't been sleeping together. At this rate, I'll be lucky if she doesn't decide to cancel the engagement and walk away from me entirely in the face of this assassination of her character. It's appalling and unforgivably rude."

"What precisely was I supposed to think, Myles? With all this cloak and dagger sneaking around, eschewing all tradition and protocol. No one even knew you were dating."

"In case you missed it, Gram, I haven't exactly let the family in on my personal life for the last decade. Why would I, when all of you have disapproved of ninety-nine percent of it since I dared to have aspirations that weren't joining the family business?"

"Don't pin your father's disappointments on the rest of us," Gram snapped.

There was so much Myles wanted to say to that, but he wasn't here to argue about old family conflicts.

"I just don't understand why you'd hide a decision this significant, unless there's something you're ashamed of."

His head was well and truly going to explode any minute now. Piper had been right. He should've introduced her first. "The only thing I'm ashamed of is your behavior. I'm proud to be able to call this kind, funny, beautiful woman mine."

Myles hoped, God how he hoped, that would still be true when they got out of here.

"Then why are you in such an all-fired hurry?"

Because I need you to sign off on the trust so I don't lose my business. He was hardly going to say that.

Myles looked at Piper beside him, standing resolute in the face of all the accusations that'd been hurled her way. Her expression said this was his call, and she'd accept whatever he decided to do.

He lifted the hand he held and pressed it over his heart. Brain scrambling for something, anything to say. "Because she makes me smile. She makes me *think.* She makes me better than I am. Because I'm thirty-one years old, and until I met Piper, I didn't even know my life was standing still. And now that I've realized it, I can't wait another month to make her a permanent part of my life." It'd started off a line, but by the time he finished, it felt like a vow. He didn't have time to analyze that just now.

Piper's eyes were huge and luminous. Her voice, when she spoke, was thick. "Well, now you're going to make me cry."

Myles brushed softly at her cheek. "Never on my account."

Someone—Piper's mother?—sighed softly.

"That's lovely. But why wouldn't you want to celebrate that with your family and friends?" Mrs. Parish asked.

Piper looked at her mom. "Because I just got finished riding the crazy train that was Carrie Jo's wedding. I went through all the hoopla for Leah's. I've been through it for half my friends. I have zero desire to waste a *year* planning something, when we want to get married now. I knew that would offend you, so we just planned to elope and surprise everyone with a party after."

Mrs. Parish huffed. "Of course, you'd ignore tradition on this, too. It's just like you." She said it with a tone of disapproval that made Myles bristle on Piper's behalf.

"Yes, it's exactly like her, and it's one of the things I appreciate most about her. She's not like anybody I've ever met."

Her mother seemed at a loss for what to say to that. Eventually she asked, "But why wouldn't you even mention you were dating?"

Piper closed her eyes and almost laughed. "Because—and I say this with love—you're nosy. Ever since Leah got married, you've been on my case, pushing and pushing and pushing after every date I went on. Does this one have possibilities? Is he the one? I couldn't even give any of them a legitimate shot because of all the pressure you were putting on me. I knew Myles was special the moment I met him. I wasn't about to let anything screw that up."

"But—" she began.

"I picked Myles. He makes me happy. That's the only thing you actually need to know." Her tone brooked no argument.

"Well, if you're dead set on eloping, I don't see why we should stand in your way," Mr. Parish said, with a look that suggested relief at not having to reprise whatever crazy he'd endured for his younger daughter's wedding.

"It's absolutely out of the question," Gram said.

Myles tensed. "I swear to God, if you say one more word about—"

"I was wrong to pry and imply things weren't above board. I apologize for that." She looked to Piper. "I really do, my dear. I'm sorry to have offended you. We've had some...difficulties in our family in the past, and I just want to protect him from making the same kind of mistake."

Piper inclined her head, a far more graceful

acknowledgment of acceptance than Myles thought his grandmother deserved.

Gram continued. "But you can't elope, Myles. As a Stewart, there are certain societal expectations you have to meet."

"Hang the expectations. I'm not waiting."

"I didn't ask you to wait. I'm asking you not to elope. If we can put together a proper wedding on the same timeline you were planning to fly off to wherever, will you agree?"

Myles opened his mouth in surprise. This he hadn't expected. "We'd need to talk about it."

Gram waved a hand. "Fine, fine. Go talk. But do it quickly. There's a great deal to do."

Piper tugged him down the hall and into a home office, shutting the door behind them.

"Jesus Christ, Piper, I'm so sorry. I—" He broke off as he noticed her lips twitching. "What on *Earth* do you have to smile about?"

"How can I not be crazy about a guy who can work trollop into a normal conversation?"

"I'm pretty sure nothing about that conversation was normal, and it seemed a better option than what Traci really was, which was a stone-cold bitch. But that's a story for another day. You aren't her. You're nothing like her. And I'm sorry my grandmother treated you like you were. I should never have dragged you into all this."

"As I recall, I've been a more than willing participant."

Myles waved a hand in the general direction of the living room. "You didn't sign up for that. I never—God. This is why I didn't want to tangle you up with my family any sooner than I had to. I'll understand if you want to pull out of the whole thing."

"You need me."

"Not at the expense of forcing you to deal with that." He'd find another way. It wasn't worth the risk of losing his chance of developing something real with Piper.

"I admit that being accused of trapping you into marriage via pregnancy was not my finest moment this week. But it's not enough to make me back out."

Relief weakened his knees. But nothing was as simple as she was trying to make it.

"I want you to think about this. Really think. Because this changes things. If we go through with this now, it's no secret. Everybody will know. We'll be married on every level. Same house, same bed, same name. It won't be as simple as you planned if things don't work out."

She studied him for several moments before turning away to face the window. Myles felt his heart sink.

"Did you mean it?" Piper turned back to look at him. "What you said about why you were marrying me?"

He couldn't lie to her. "Every word. I hope that doesn't freak you out. I know it's a lot and it's soon and—"

She crossed the room in two strides and pressed her lips softly to his. "It's nice to know I'm not the only one on this crazy train." Her fingers combed through his hair. "I want to marry you, Myles. For real. I want to live with you and wake up with you and take your name.

And while your grandmother kind of terrifies me, maybe we should take her up on her offer. It might pacify everybody, and we need her on your side."

"Sure?" He knew a full-blown wedding wasn't what she wanted.

"Positive."

They grinned at each other.

"You're aware you're unleashing the kraken, right?"

Her mouth quirked. "Yeah."

"Okay then."

The living room was strangely silent as they came back, still hand-in-hand. Myles sighed and worked up a smile for his grandmother. "Well, it looks like you're planning a wedding."

WHAT DID a girl wear to meet her prospective in-laws?

Piper stood in her closet, pondering that question, knowing she needed to pick something and finish getting ready for the engagement dinner.

Yesterday had been hideous. Mortifying. Infuriating. She'd never been so embarrassed in her life as when Suzanne Stewart had calmly asked how far along she was. Her parents, rather than jumping to immediate denials or objections had just *looked* at her.

Right, because she was *that* girl? Who would've thought that their silence could take a bigger piece of her than all the years of little jibes and digs. She'd always known she was a disappointment to them, but she'd never have imagined they'd believe that of her. It was a harsh blow to their already strained relationship.

And Myles had come to her rescue like an avenging angel in flannel and jeans. No hesitation. She'd never seen him angry before. Seeing it, not because his own plans stood to be derailed but on her behalf, had been magnificent. But Piper wasn't exactly in the mood for a reprisal tonight. As it drew near to time to go, her nerves began to jitter. Would the rest of Myles' family be that...judgmental? In all their intensive getting to know each other the past week and a half, he'd been relatively close-lipped about them, saying only that he was the black sheep. If his parents and siblings were anything like his grandmother, no wonder he never went home.

In two weeks, she'd be legally tied to these people. If this lunacy blew up in her face, there'd be no quiet extrication from the situation. She wouldn't be just facing his family. She'd be facing everyone she knew, permanently marked as having failed. Divorce hadn't seemed like that big a deal when it'd been on the down low, but now...

Selecting a classic little black dress that managed to be both conservative and sexy, Piper slipped into it. She opted for the knee-high bitch boots. The three-inch heels would give her an extra boost of confidence, along with some height. Her pearls came next—the necklace and matching earrings from her own grandmother. Then the engagement ring Myles had given her in a blanket fort.

Piper laid a hand on her fluttering belly.

There'd be no easing into this. They were about to jump into the deep end of the pool in front of a very wide, very public audience. That'd seemed like a glorious, even romantic idea yesterday, in the wake of his admission.

Until I met Piper, I didn't even know my life was standing still. And now that I've realized it, I can't wait another month to make her a permanent part of my life.

It wasn't love exactly. But it had the potential to be, and her romantic heart had wanted to take the leap with him. Because being with him helped fill in some of the chinks left by years of trying to fit in with her family.

Now she wondered if she was in over her head. Was she making a foolish decision because she was carried away in that heady, new relationship infatuation? Was it a bad sign that she felt panicked when she wasn't actually with her husband-to-be?

Husband. Jesus.

In two weeks—no, less—ten days, she'd be walking down the aisle to him. Why did that seem so much bigger than a little courthouse ceremony?

Because having all her family and friends there made it real. Not a role. Not a sort of pretend, with the option to play house if they felt like it. A real marriage. That was absolutely terrifying. Not because she didn't want him, but because she was afraid they wouldn't survive it. They weren't strangers. They'd been friends, co-stars. And now they were very definitely more. But would it be enough?

The bell rang.

Piper took one last look at herself in the bathroom mirror, cleaning up a tiny mascara smudge, and said, "Show time." Then she went to answer the door.

Myles took a deep breath and gave her an appreciative once over that made the angsting over her outfit completely worth it. "If I were a cartoon wolf, my eyes would be bugging out like telescopes right now, with a big horn going AHOOOOGAH."

And just like that, the knots in her belly loosened. She offered him a smile. "I do aim to please. But seriously, is this okay for meeting your parents?"

"More than. Although you could wear a gunny sack, and I wouldn't have a problem with it."

"It's not you I'm worried about."

"Nervous?" he asked, stepping inside.

"A little. It was one thing to just show up after the deed was done. 'Hi, I'm your new daughter-in-law.' It's quite another to go the more traditional route, albeit in fast forward."

"We don't need their approval."

"Doesn't change the desire to have it." She reached out to straighten his tie, not because it needed it, but just for an excuse to touch him. "Like it or not, our families are part of our lives and tonight we're both running the gauntlet with all of them."

Myles slid his hands over her hips, pulling

her closer. "Partners in crime, remember? We're in this together. And I really want to kiss you now, but I don't want to mess up your makeup."

"Smudge-proof," she said. "I really wanted to kiss you, too."

"I love a forward-thinking woman," he grinned, bending his head to hers.

An edge of stark heat underscored the playful tangle of tongues. Myles let out a groan that rumbled his chest against hers. It was tempting—so tempting—to fall into the kiss and lose themselves. But responsibilities awaited.

Piper stepped back, lips still tingling. "We have places to be."

"More's the pity." His eyes, deep and dark, looked her up and down again. "Because all I really want to do is peel you out of that dress. You can keep the boots. Because I really, really like the boots."

An image of what he could do to her while she wore nothing but her bitch boots planted itself in her brain and bloomed. Warmth pooled between her thighs. Searching for a release of the tension, she sent him a sassy grin. "If you're a very good boy, maybe I'll bring them on the honeymoon."

"Mmm, the honeymoon. Yes, please." He angled his head. "Speaking of, given the rapidly approaching nature of our nuptials, are we waiting?"

Well, he was just putting that right out there. She blew out a shaky breath. "If things were different, I'd be dragging you back to the bedroom by your tie already. But given how jam-packed the next week or so is going to be, I don't know that there'd be the time either of us would prefer to devote to that particular pursuit. So yeah, I think maybe we are."

"Fair point. And I have to admit, there's something kind of primal and appealing about the idea of claiming you as my wife."

Well, God. Piper's legs went lax, every nerve in her body standing up to scream *oh yes* at the images that invoked.

Myles smiled, a rather smug curve of lips

that told her he knew exactly where her brain was. The bastard. He was going to spend the next ten days torturing them both, and Piper had a feeling it was going to be glorious.

THE DRIVE to Tosca didn't take long, but they were still the last to arrive. Myles' entire family was booked to stay that night at The Babylon, the new hotel and spa just down the street. The group gathered around Suzanne at a high-top table in the bar must be them. Piper's own parents, sister, brother-in-law, and—dear God, why had they brought a two-year-old to an engagement dinner?—hovered to one side of the lobby.

"Everybody in their own corners, I suppose," she observed.

"Can't blame them after yesterday," Myles murmured. "Once more into the breach."

Leah spotted them first. "Here they are!" she crooned, already crossing over, Preston on her hip. "Oh, he is just gorgeous and I can't believe you've been keeping him a secret all this time. Let me see the ring," she gushed.

Already wishing her sister would take a breath, Piper held out her hand.

"Wow. Just wow." She shot an impressed look at Myles. "You did good. I'm Leah Cramer, by the way. Baby sis. And this is Preston. Pres, this is going to be your Uncle Myles."

"Pie," Preston said, stretching his chubby little arms out for Piper.

Myles chuckled. "I think he's more interested in dessert."

"No, I'm Pie." Piper handed Myles her clutch and reached for her nephew.

"She's his absolute favorite thing," Leah said, handing him over.

Preston immediately latched on like a monkey, pressing his sticky cheek to Piper's. "Pie," he said happily.

As the adoration was completely mutual, she snuggled him to her while Leah continued the introductions.

"This is my husband, Elliott. And I believe you've met our parents, Twyla and Paul."

Myles shook hands all around, wisely not mentioning the circumstances of their first meeting.

Piper bounced Preston on her hip. "Hey buddy. Can you say hi to Myles?"

He shifted around in Piper's arms and fixed solemn blue eyes on Myles. Myles bent down a bit to get on Preston's level, offering his hand. "Hey there. Pie's my favorite, too."

Preston giggled and gave Myles a toothy grin. "Pie!" He let go of Piper and leaned toward Myles.

"Oh. Well, apparently that was the magic phrase." Piper tried to shift him back to a better position before he fell, but Myles plucked him up and settled him on his own hip, her clutch tucked under his arm.

"No worries. We Pie-men must stick to-gether, right Preston?"

The sight of Myles with her nephew perched comfortably in one arm made something in Piper's chest feel funny. She watched him attempt to teach Preston to fist bump and tried to catch her breath. Leah and Twyla exchanged pleased looks.

"You look good with a kid, big brother."

The sound of another woman's voice shook Piper out of her daze.

The Stewart clan had come out of the bar to join them. At the head of the pack was a young woman a few inches taller than Piper, with Myles' caramel eyes and a ready smile.

"Yeah, well, don't get ahead of yourself," Myles said. "Nobody's in a hurry here."

"Says the guy getting married in ten days. I'm Skye. And of course, you're Piper. I've heard so much about you!" Skye pulled Piper into a warm hug.

"You have?" Piper cut her eyes toward Myles, wondering what he'd said.

"Of course, this sneaky devil played it off like you weren't dating during the show. I totally didn't believe him. Your chemistry was way too good. The show was amazing, by the way."

"Oh, I didn't realize you came," Piper said faintly.

"Suzanne, Skye, and I did. It was wonderful. I had no idea my boy could act." An older version of Skye stepped forward, her dark hair swept up in a classic chignon.

"I could always act," Myles protested.

She shot him a pitying look. "Not based on the stories you told to cover up your shenanigans growing up. I'm Augusta Stewart, Myles' mother. Welcome to the family." She, too, stepped in for a hug, pressing her cheek to Piper's as she whispered, "I'm sorry about my mother-in-law."

"Thank you," Piper murmured.

"And this is my husband, Warrick, and Myles' brother, Grady," Augusta said.

No more than handshakes and reserved nods from the other Stewart men. Grady was, as Myles had told her, a younger, carbon copy of their father. They were so unlike Myles with his energy and enthusiasm, it was hard to believe he came from the same family.

Apparently picking up on her surprise, he leaned in to whisper, "We aren't a demonstrative bunch. It's not dignified."

Piper would take his lack of dignity and sense of humor any day.

The hostess hung back as the rest of the introductions were made between the two families. Everyone was cordial and the younger women, at least, seemed determined to be cheerful and make up for the antagonism of the previous day.

Well, better than a cat fight.

"If you'll come this way, your table is ready."

Myles relinquished Preston back to his mother and pressed a hand against the small of Piper's back. "So far, so good."

Piper found herself between Myles and Skye, across from her sister and brother-in-law. As seating arrangements went, it was far better than being right next to Suzanne. Piper wasn't quite ready to share space with the other woman. General small talk got them through perusal of the menu, but once their orders were taken, talk inevitably turned to the wedding.

"What are you thinking, Piper?" Skye asked.

Small and intimate, beachside and barefoot. Just Myles and me and the minister... But, of course, she wouldn't get that. It wouldn't fit Suzanne's requirement for a societal splash.

"I don't know. An actual wedding wasn't what we'd had planned, and I'm not entirely sure what can be pulled together in so little time."

"I'm already working on that," Suzanne announced. "Ceremony will be rooftop at The Babylon under the pergola, with reception to follow in the ballroom below. In the event of rain—not currently in the forecast—the ceremony can be moved inside. I'm meeting with the hotel caterers tomorrow. You and Myles have an appointment with Carolanne Wheeler at Sweet Magnolias Bakery to pick a cake tomorrow at twelve-thirty. Brides and Belles is on standby, waiting for measurements for the men. Piper, how many attendants will you have?"

"I…" She trailed off, staring at Suzanne in shock. "You did all that in thirty-six hours?"

"There are still hundreds of details to figure out and finalize. Attendants?"

"I haven't even asked them yet." *Haven't even told them I'm getting married. I should get on that.*

"For heaven's sake, get with the program. We have ten days."

"Gram…" Myles warned.

But she ignored him. "I'll have itineraries ready for the two of you tomorrow."

"Itineraries," Piper repeated.

"I told you we'd unleashed the kraken," Myles whispered.

"No kidding."

"I need to see your dress before I meet with the florist, so I have a notion of style."

"I haven't got one yet."

"You don't have *a dress*?" Suzanne asked, aghast.

"I didn't need one to elope.

"Well, we have to find you a dress ASAP," Leah said.

"I suppose I'll order something classic and we'll decide on a style of bouquet once you have the gown."

"The flowers should be bold," Myles spoke up. "Something with a lot of pop and color, to match the bride."

Suzanne wagged a finger at him. "Your job is not to opine, young man. It's to show up when and where you're told. Planning a wedding in ten days isn't for the faint of heart."

"It was *your* idea," he pointed out.

"Not that we're not grateful," Piper rushed to add.

"Suzanne, what can we do to help?" Twyla asked.

Conversation shifted back to the other end of the table.

"I feel a little like I've been hit by a wrecking ball," Piper admitted.

"You get used to it."

"Gram will get the wedding taken care of. I

want to know where you're going on your honeymoon," Skye said. "Somewhere fabulous, I hope."

"We haven't even talked about it yet. We're in the dead center of cold and flu season at work, and Myles can't be away from the paper for very long just now."

He hadn't said that, but with the deadline for paying back the loan looming, she was certain that would be the case. They'd need to be local to jump through whatever hoops were required to gain access to the trust.

"We'd already made arrangements to get away for the long weekend to elope. So, I figured we'd take the weekend, go somewhere not too far—maybe New Orleans. Then later on this year, when things slow down for both of us at work, we'll go somewhere awesome for a proper honeymoon."

"You'd have the flexibility to take a proper honeymoon for as long as you liked if you gave up this ridiculous newspaper and took your proper place at the company," Warrick said.

Beside her, Myles stiffened.

Piper laid her hand on his thigh in warning. "Myles has brought that newspaper back from the brink and re-invigorated it as a center of the community and a beacon of hope. He's become a central part of everyone's life here in Wishful, bringing us the news that matters."

"News that matters?" Warrick scoffed. "Reports of parades and volunteer work and local land squabbles are hardly earth-shattering events."

"He recognizes what all good journalists do —that people matter. People are the heart, the truth of any story. Not the sensationalist yellow journalism that seems to be running rampant in the rest of the country. So, regardless of your opinion of his endeavor, Mr. Stewart, let me assure you that he's goddamned amazing at what he does, and I don't for a second begrudge delaying a 'proper' honeymoon so that he can continue to do it."

Twyla made a choking noise, but Piper didn't stop to catch the familiar flash of appalled disappointment on her face. Color crept up Warrick's face during Piper's little rant and he opened his mouth to say something, but his mother interrupted.

"You've found a woman with spine. Good for you, Myles." Suzanne nodded in approval, then sat back as their food was served.

"Piper."

Braced for censure, she looked at Myles. "I'm sorry, I just couldn't sit here and let him—"

He cupped her jaw and pressed his lips softly to hers. A thank you. A promise. And maybe something more.

"How do you feel about Greece?"

"Greece?" she asked dumbly.

"Or the French Riviera. I kind of don't care where, as long as it involves you and a bikini."

She cleared her throat, feeling the heat in her own cheeks. "I'm sure we can work something out."

CHAPTER 6

"WES, I NEED YOU to follow up on the current status of negotiations between Bill Covey and Lloyd MacIntosh about the Chapel Springs development. Simone, you need to set up an interview with Margot Thayer over at The Babylon. They're past the soft opening of the spa and I want to do a feature on all the available services, and plans for additional expansion in the works. Take Zach with you, since you haven't met her yet. Get pics of some of the treatments that'll make people want to sign up. And since you're already seeing Omar, make sure you get his column for the Sunday edition." Myles absently twisted at the Rubik's cube in his hands as he checked his list.

The conference room door swung open and his grandmother swept in with all the pomp of Queen Elizabeth, sans entourage.

Patty, looking harried, brought up the rear. "Sorry, Myles. I tried to stop her."

"It's fine, Patty. What can I do for you, Gram?"

Clearly in no mood for small talk, she launched right in. "I've already told you: Be where you're told, when you're told. You've got a tux fitting at 4:30."

Myles opened his mouth to say he couldn't make a 4:30 appointment, then closed it again as his grandmother rolled right on.

"I've already met with the caterers this morning. Without a guest list, there's no way to do a proper sit-down dinner, so it'll be buffet." This she said with the faint sneer she reserved for anything she deemed as improper. "I'll need an estimated number of those expected to attend on the bride's side."

"Yes ma'am."

Simone held up a hand. "I'm sorry. Bride? Tux? Why does it sound like you're getting married?"

"Because I am. A week from Saturday."

"To who?" Patty asked, agape.

"Piper Parish."

"Seriously?" Wes goggled at him.

"Yes, yes, and there's still so much to do," Gram said. "There's no florist in this town. How can there be no florist?"

"Well, there used to be, but nobody was around to take over after Francine passed about six years ago because her protégé, Wynne Montgomery, moved off to New Orleans," Patty said.

Gram waved that away. "I've got calls in to Whitley's and Martha Haverford. And I've still got to find a photographer. I haven't been able to reach the one listed here."

"That's because he's been sitting in a

meeting with me all morning," Myles said. "Zach, you busy next Saturday?"

"Nothing I can't rearrange."

Myles turned back to his grandmother. "There. Photographer. Done."

"Honestly, Myles. As if it's that simple. Young man, I'll need to schedule an appointment as soon as possible to go over your portfolio to see if you meet with our expectations."

"I can make time this afternoon, but—" Zach began.

"Excellent. See that you do. Myles will give you my contact information."

"Uh, okay."

Myles mouthed a *Sorry* as Gram opened her purse and pulled out two folders. "Here's the current itinerary. Please pass a copy to Piper when you see her at the cake tasting. You do remember you're due at the bakery for the cake tasting in twenty minutes?"

"Yes ma'am. I remember."

Her cell phone rang. She whipped it out of her purse and answered. "Yes Elaine. No, I'm glad you got back to me. My grandson is getting married." Gram tipped the phone away from her mouth. "Four-thirty," she hissed, before walking out as quickly as she'd come.

Myles' entire staff stared at him. "So, I'm getting married," he said.

"And we're just hearing about this now, why?" Patty asked.

"You wouldn't have been hearing about it at all, until after the fact, if Piper and I had had our way, but our families threw a fit when they found out we were eloping."

"You and Piper. Wow." Zach crossed his arms. "Didn't call that."

"The unsung romance from *White Christmas*. We skated under the radar thanks to all the drama with Tyler and Brody."

"You need engagement pictures?"

"I'm sure Gram will say we do. I'll touch base with Piper and see when we can squeeze them in. And listen, please don't take offense at her. She's like a five-star general leading a campaign when she gets into event planning mode."

"I see now where you get it," he said.

"Get what?"

"Your style of getting things done."

Before Myles could think of a reply to that, Wes began to hum "The Wedding March".

Piper walked into the conference room, attention still down the hall. "Why do I get the sense that if the President appointed her a cabinet member, she'd manage to straighten out everything wrong with the government inside a month?"

"Probably because she could if she put her mind to it." Gram, of all members of his family, was the one most likely to follow words with action. She was, he supposed, where he'd learned that.

"Your grandmother is a scary, scary woman."

"And my bride is a very frazzled one."

Piper's face was a little wan, and her hair, which had been pulled up into a knot at the back of her head, stuck out at odd angles. "Does it show?"

His lips twitched. "Well, it looks like you started to run your fingers through your hair and then got stuck."

She reached up and patted her hair. "Oh hell. No wonder your grandmother was giving me a death glare. She'll probably have me booked for a total makeover when I'm supposed to be giving breathing treatments and steroid shots."

"About that. We have itineraries."

She made a pained face. "How bad?"

"I haven't looked yet, but I'm sure we don't get to sleep for the next nine days. Do you actually have time for this cake tasting?"

"If you don't, I expect we'd all be happy to take a field trip to taste stuff for you," Zach offered.

"Seriously, we really support cake," Wes said.

The corners of Piper's mouth fluttered into a tired smile. "I really *don't* have time, but we're calling it lunch. Otherwise I won't get a chance to eat. We're slammed today."

"Cake for lunch. I can get behind that. Just

let me finish up here. You want to go wait in my office?"

"I'll go do something about…this." She gestured to her head, then offered a tired smile to his staff. "Sorry to interrupt."

"Not at all, honey. And congratulations!" said Patty.

Everyone else echoed the sentiment and Piper headed down the hall, itinerary in hand.

Myles got updates on various outstanding stories, finished handing out assignments, and added to his list of things to check on for the next edition.

"One thing we'll need to discuss is division of labor while I'm gone. I don't anticipate being out of the office for more than a few days, but I'd feel better having a plan in place while I am."

"What? You're not going on a honeymoon?" Wes asked.

"We're just taking a long weekend for the wedding and a couple days away. The honeymoon will come later when work slows down for us both."

"And when does work ever slow down for you?" Patty wanted to know.

"I have aspirations for later this year, once Simone knows all the ropes here and we can, hopefully, bring in some more help. Circulation is going up, and I think that trend will continue, so I'm optimistic we'll actually be in a position to do that."

"Here's to that." Simone lifted her coffee cup in a toast.

"Anyway, once I have a chance to go over the itinerary, I'll have a better idea what I'll need someone to cover, so we'll talk about that later. Meanwhile, there is cake calling my name. Dismissed."

Piper was sprawled in a chair in his office, hair still a mess, a frown bowing those lovely lips.

"What's wrong?"

She held up the itinerary. "This. It's so...so... We're being put on display, Myles."

"It's an unfortunate side effect of marrying a Stewart, I'm afraid."

"I was hoping for something small and intimate. Close friends and family. This is... I don't even know what this is."

Myles pulled her out of the chair and into his arms. "It's Gram being Gram. I'll talk to her, do my best to rein her in some. Or I can get her to put on the brakes entirely and we can go back to our original plan and elope."

"I don't think there's any putting this genie back in the bottle. She's already spent who knows how much in deposits getting stuff lined up at the last minute. The last thing I want is for us to piss her off and you risk losing access to the trust. I'm not going to let you lose the paper because I'm being pissy and picky over details that won't matter after the fact."

Myles ran his hands down her arms. "Do you still want this wedding?"

"You need—"

"I don't care what I need. Do you still want to do this? It's more than you signed on for."

Piper reached up to frame his face. "I signed on for you. To help you, yes, but at the end of the day, Myles, I want you. Period. If that means I have to be a show pony for the next nine days, I'll do it."

Myles sighed, lowering his brow to hers. "What did I do to deserve you?"

"You made me a blanket fort."

"If that's all it takes to make you happy, I'll have one permanently installed at the house."

Someone knocked on the door frame, and Myles realized the door was wide open. Simone stood in the doorway. "Didn't y'all have somewhere to be?"

"Oh, crap. Let me go run a brush through my hair. Two minutes!" Piper snatched her purse and raced down the hall to the bathroom.

Myles eyed Simone, struggling to keep his face impassive. Had she heard about the threat to the paper?

"Patty managed to get the interview moved to accommodate your tux fitting," she said.

"Thank God. Pretty sure Piper wouldn't care if I was waiting at the end of the aisle in my favorite jeans and Chucks, but Gram would have a coronary."

Simone hesitated.

"There something else?"

She shook her head. "Nothing that can't wait. You're going to be late."

Piper rushed back in, her hair neatened up and her makeup freshened.

"Okay, I'm ready. Let's rock and roll, Mr. Stewart. My blood sugar has tanked and there is cake calling my name."

"As you wish, milady." With a worried glance at Simone, he grabbed his coat and his keys, and followed his bride-to-be out the door.

"Was that the last of them?" Miranda asked.

Shelby peeked into the waiting room. "Looks like."

"Quick. Lock the door before anybody else sneaks in."

Piper crossed to the front door and flipped

the lock. "We are officially *closed*. Thank God."

"I'm out. There is a pot roast in my future. Night." Shelby nabbed her purse from a drawer and scurried out the back door.

"That was just mean," Piper said. "Taunting us with pot roast and not offering to share."

"It does bring home the salient point that I require food. I don't think I've had anything since those cupcakes you brought back from lunch," Miranda said.

The thought of cake made Piper vaguely sick. So. Many. Flavors. So. Much. Sugar. But she and Myles had agreed completely on the red velvet. Because chocolate. Duh. Her hubby-to-be had quite the sweet tooth, as it turned out.

"I'm thinking Chinese," Miranda continued. "If I order enough I won't have to cook for a couple of days."

"I'll see your Chinese and raise you beer and chili fries from The Mudcat," Piper said.

"Ooo, chili fries. If you twist my arm, I could probably be persuaded."

"Good because Norah, Tyler, and Tucker are already meeting us there."

Miranda slid off her white coat and hung it up. "Did I forget somebody's birthday?"

"No. I have news and it's easier to share when everybody's together." And as much as she wanted to go home and fall face first into bed, it needed to be shared tonight before they heard it from other sources.

"Okay, okay, you've twisted my arm. Meet you there."

Piper thought about making a detour home to change out of her scrubs, but there was too great a temptation to find a soft horizontal surface, so she pointed her car toward downtown. Her phone rang as she was pulling out of the lot, Myles' name flashing on the caller ID.

"If you're calling to tell me your grandmother has somewhere else for us to be, I'm not coming."

"No word from The Kraken. But I am going to be late. The tux fitting ran long and I've got a snarl to work out at the paper before I'm free."

"Do you want me to wait for you?'"

"Don't know how long I'll be, so go ahead and tell them. The longer you're sitting in public, the more likely someone will have heard and come up to congratulate you before you get a chance to make the announcement."

"Given the volume of people who rotated through the clinic today, it's a minor miracle it hasn't happened already."

"Didn't slow down any after cake?"

Piper groaned. "Do not mention cake to me. I am not touching cake again until you feed it to me at the reception."

He chuckled softly. "I told you, you should've stopped for a sandwich or something."

"Yeah, well, I'll be rectifying the or something in short order. You want me to go ahead and order you anything?"

"Nah. I'll order when I get there. I can always mooch off your plate until my food arrives."

Piper gasped in mock surprise. "You're a

moocher? Well, now, I don't know if I can marry a moocher."

"I'm a moocher who shares."

"Oh, I suppose that's all right then. See you soon."

"I'll be there as soon as I can."

Piper thought about slipping on the ring before going inside, but pulling it out and putting it on when she told them made such a nice dramatic statement. She had no idea how they'd react. Tyler and Tucker in particular knew she'd made her vow to swear off Myles for three months after the end of the show. Announcing she was engaged to him barely a week after that expired was bound to raise a few eyebrows and concerns. She didn't like lying to them. But it seemed more sensible to stick to the story they'd told their families. That they'd been together since the show started.

The Mudcat Tavern was hopping. Patrons huddled around tables, standing two-deep at the bar or in lines around the dart boards. The latest game in March Madness played on several TV screens, though none of the commentary could be heard over the din of people. Tucker waved from a booth in the back. As he ran his own law practice, he'd had the flexibility to get out before the rest of them and stake claim on a table.

Piper made her way through the crowd, deliberately not meeting anyone's gaze or inviting the usual chitchat and conversation. She slid into the booth opposite him and immediately snagged his beer for a swig.

Tucker's brows arched up. "That kind of day, huh?"

"Oh yes. Don't worry. I've practically showered in disinfectant."

"Keep it. I'll get another." He studied her. "So...what's this news you have to share?"

"Nope. Not spilling until everybody is here. Having to repeat myself ruins the dramatic punch." Which was something of an untruth. The news itself was so shocking, she doubted anything would dim the punch.

"Does this have something to do with why

you've been MIA for the last couple of weeks?"

"Yes."

Miranda slid in next, grabbed the beer from Piper and took a long pull herself.

"I'll just go get a pitcher." Tucker rose and headed for the bar.

By the time he made it back, juggling a pitcher and several glasses, Norah and Tyler had arrived.

"I feel like I'm interrupting a hen party," he said. "Where's Cam?"

"At a City Council meeting," Norah announced.

"You didn't have to be there, too?" Piper asked. As the city planner, Norah worked closely with her fiancé, City Councilman Campbell Crawford.

"Not tonight."

"Well, it wouldn't be a total hen party if Brody wasn't in Portland," Piper pointed out.

"He'll be home next weekend," Tyler said. "Two more months on this project and then he's all mine."

After years apart, Tyler and Brody had come back together during the production of *White Christmas* that had saved The Madrigal Theater —with some creative manipulation on the part of Piper, Tucker, and Myles. He'd had one last job to take as project coordinator for Peyton Consolidated before he was free to come home to Wishful permanently and open his own construction firm.

"Okay, everybody's here," Tucker said. "Spill it, Parish. What's going on?"

Suddenly nervous, Piper rolled her glass between both hands. "I have news. Well, and a confession."

"Oh, please God, tell me you haven't taken another better paying job somewhere else," Miranda said, looking stricken.

"What? No. Nothing like that."

"It's good news," Norah declared, a grin spreading across her face.

Piper pointed at her. "You know. How do you know? Who told you?"

Before she could answer, Tyler interrupted,

"How about you just tell us whatever it is you're being squirrelly about?"

"Okay, fine. So, when I made that whole big deal about not dating my co-star and giving time for the intimacy of the stage to wear off after the show? I was full of crap. Myles and I have been dating. Secretly."

"Why secretly? It's not like any of us have a problem with him," Tyler said.

"Because you were there when I did the same thing with Brandon, and I didn't want any reminders of how that blew up in my face." Which was a half-truth. Not wanting those reminders was one of the few things that had allowed her to keep her personal vow of distance.

"So, you hauled us all out tonight to come clean about the fact that you're dating a guy you've clearly liked since the day you met?" Tyler asked. "Give us a little credit, Piper. We're not going to judge you for that. For God's sake, Brody and I fell in love on the stage. It happens."

Norah bit her lip, obviously trying to hold

in a grin.

"No, the fact that Myles and I have been dating was the preamble." She reached back to unfasten the clasp of the chain, pulling the necklace free of her shirt and sliding the ring onto her finger. "I dragged you all out tonight because Myles and I are getting married."

"Woo!" Norah did a fist pump. "I've been sitting on that all afternoon. If you hadn't called, I would've tracked you down at home."

"How is it you knew all afternoon and nobody told me," Tyler complained.

"You run the hardware store," said Norah. "Relationship gossip is less what gets brought to you. Whereas I have a coffee habit that also happens to coincide with my daily gossip fuel up. And today that meant Cassie telling me she heard it from Carolanne that you had a cake tasting."

"Wow, congrats!" Miranda leaned in for a hug. "This is awesome. Wait, why did you have a cake tasting today?"

"Because the wedding is a week from

Saturday."

"What?!" Tyler exploded. "Okay that came out wrong. Why so fast?"

"We were going to just elope—that was our preference—but his grandmother found out and had a hissy fit. We said we didn't want to wait, thinking she'd be put off, but nope. She's putting together a wedding in ten days. She's the only person I've ever met other than Norah who could actually pull that off. It's kind of ter-rifying."

"Well I think it's great," Norah declared. "You two were great together on stage. It only makes sense that you'd be great in real life. Gotta say, though, I'm jealous you're going to pull off your wedding before me. We had to schedule ours so far out from the engagement to get ahead of the city calendar, it's starting to feel like it's never going to happen."

"Elopement has a lot going for it. I'm just sayin'. I still wish that's what we were doing, but the families are involved now, so it's no longer about us."

"Is *this* about you?" Tucker asked. He'd been strangely silent since she'd made the announcement, and now he looked uncharacteristically grave.

"What kind of question is that? Of course it's about us. What else would it be about?"

But Piper could tell by the look on his face that he knew. Of course, he knew. He was Myles' attorney. He knew about the trust. He was the one who'd made the crack about Vegas.

Tucker just shook his head. "Nothing. I just want you to be happy."

She laid a hand over his and squeezed. "I am. Although my level of happiness would be dramatically improved by a bacon cheeseburger and onion rings." Looking around, she flagged a waitress.

They placed their orders. As soon as the waitress hurried away, Piper turned to her friends. "Okay, so please tell me the three of you are available to go dress shopping tomorrow."

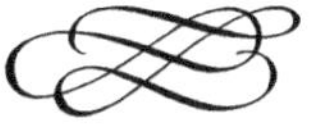

CHAPTER 7

"THERE! THE DAMNED THING is fixed." Myles tossed a small basketball toward the hoop mounted on the wall, giving a celebratory fist pump on the swish. "There is beer and a burger in my future."

Before he could make a beeline for the exit, Simone shut the door to his office, her face serious. "Is there something you want to tell me?"

The answer is 'No, absolutely not.' "You're doing a kick ass job. Which you already know."

She angled her head, eyes narrowed in disapproval. That wasn't what she'd meant and they both knew it.

"What did Piper mean that you could lose the paper?"

Shit.

"The paper's fine." It wasn't a lie. With his marriage and access to the trust, it would be within a month.

"Myles, I've known you too long. You're an old friend and I changed my whole life to come up here and work with you. You owe me the truth if that's about to blow up in my face."

Editor Busted For Lying To His Staff, Forced To Come Clean

Myles scrubbed both hands over his face, feeling the rasp of beard stubble against his palms. He was too damned tired for this. But she was right. He owed her the truth.

"Okay, look. I had to pursue unconventional investment when I bought the paper. My investor has decided to pull out early, and I owe the balance of the loan by May 4th or my ownership of the paper is forfeit."

"Myles! Are you in it with some kind of loan shark?"

He smiled a little. Given the stories they'd covered back when he worked in The Big Easy, the question wasn't entirely out of left field. "No. Nothing illegal. And it's not a problem. My grandfather left me a trust."

"Why didn't you use the money from that to buy the paper in the first place?"

That certainly would've been handy. "I don't gain access to it until I'm married."

Her eyes widened. "Dear God, tell me you didn't just ask Piper to marry you for this. I know you haven't turned into that kind of asshole."

"No. Actually, the whole thing was Piper's idea."

"*She* thought you should have this out of the blue wedding just to save the paper?" Skepticism dripped from her voice.

"My girl loves a crazy plan." He explained how the whole thing had come about.

"That's messed up, Myles."

"Little bit," he agreed. "But I'm not going to lose the paper, so set your mind at ease."

"I hope you know what you're doing."

"Me too. And listen, keep that to yourself. I don't want anyone worrying needlessly."

She nodded. "Fine. But keep me in the loop. If something goes wrong…"

Myles crossed to Simone and took her shoulders. "Nothing's going wrong."

"Right. You're getting *married* in eight days to a woman lunatic enough to think this was a good idea. What could go wrong?"

"Don't say that. It's temping the fates. I've got to get on. Piper's waiting for me." It struck him then, that after next week, she'd be waiting for him every night. What would it be like going home to something other than silence and solitude? Because Myles was confident life with Piper would never lend itself to something so mundane as silence. Life with her would never, ever be boring.

On the short drive to The Mudcat, Myles decided he could do with a little boring after all the drama this week. He hoped he wasn't about to walk into more of it. Over the last several months, he'd become friends with most of her friends because of the show and because Wishful was a small town. But he really didn't know how they'd respond to the news. Surely if Piper ran into trouble, she'd text or call another 911 like she had when Gram showed up.

A wave of sound hit him when he walked into the bar. Some days he loved this. The noise, the sound of people. Today wasn't one of those days. But no way was he leaving Piper to fend for herself. They were in this together. Resolute, he made his way through the throngs of people, until he spotted her in a booth in the back. The fatigue slid away at the sight of her smiling and laughing with the others.

One more week and that smile would be waiting for him every night.

I am a lucky S.O.B.

"Please tell me the three of you are available to go dress shopping tomorrow. Because if you don't go, then it'll be just my mom and Leah and maybe Myles' scary grandmother to make sure I don't pick anything that will embarrass the family. I need allies."

"You've got one in me," Myles said, sliding into the booth beside her. "I'll have the minister add that to my vows. Love, honor, and protect from scary grandmother. Only fair since you ripped my dad a new one at the engagement dinner."

Piper wrinkled her nose adorably. "He deserved it. And you can't come. You aren't allowed to see the dress. Also—" She grabbed a fistful of his shirt and tugged him forward for a kiss.

Myles felt the last strain of the day bleed out.

She grinned. "Hi."

He grinned back, loving that she was a little bit breathless. "Hi yourself."

"You get everything straightened out?"

"Yeah, it's all set. Everything okay here?" He shifted his gaze to the others.

Norah was fairly bouncing with excitement.

Given she'd been planning her own wedding for the past several months, she was absolutely in that mode. Miranda, whom he didn't know well, seemed amused more than anything else.

"I understand congratulations are in order." Tyler's brows were arched as she looked from Piper to him.

"Congratulations? No threats? Attempts to talk us out of it? Lectures on practicality and the way things are supposed to be done?"

"Please. I've known Piper since we were in diapers. Any of that would fall on deaf ears. Besides, given the role *you* played last fall in getting Brody and me back together, I can only assume you're a kindred spirit and perfect for her. Sneaky bastard." Her smile took the sting out.

Myles laughed. "I'll take that as a compliment."

Tucker, who'd remained silent, tipped back the last of his beer. "Can I have a word with you in private? There's been a new development in that matter I was handling for you."

Myles doubted that. "Oh?"

"Some new information has come to light that might change things."

Translation: *I have things to say to you that I'm not going to say in front of the others.*

Fine.

They slid out of the booth and headed for the patio door.

Tucker rounded on him as soon as they stepped outside. "What the hell, Myles? When I said that about Vegas, I was making a *joke.* I did not intend for you to go out and propose to one of my closest friends in the name of getting access to the money."

Here was the objection he'd been braced for.

He kept his voice even. "My relationship with Piper is none of your business."

"*What* relationship? You don't have a relationship. Or you didn't before a week and a half ago. I don't care what she said about you dating in secret. I've known Piper all my life. I know when she's lying."

No sense in contradicting him. "Can you

blame her? She's already had to deal with both our families losing their shit. She really didn't want to deal with it from y'all, too."

Tucker stared. "Is that supposed to make me feel better? I swear to God, if I wasn't bound by attorney-client privilege, I'd be telling her exactly what was behind this grand gesture."

Though he'd expected this, Myles found himself pissed off that someone else who called him friend would think he'd use Piper in the name of saving his own ass.

"There's nothing you can tell her that she doesn't already know. I told her everything. Including your joke about Vegas. I never dreamed she'd suggest we get married."

Tucker's mouth fell open, his head of steam escaping as his assumptions got turned upside down. Myles had to feel a little bit of gratification at seeing the other man speechless, when he'd been so certain who was in the wrong.

Tucker shoved a hand through his blond hair and heaved a sigh. "We're talking about the woman who convinced me to fake a broken leg so Brody had to step in as understudy and Tyler would have to talk to him again. Piper loves lunatic schemes."

"I know. It's one of my favorite things about her."

"But you *should have said no,* not gone and put a ring on her finger. She's made it through life this far without one of her plans blowing up on her because she had the rest of us to be voices of reason."

"I'd think the ring would go a fair way toward proving that I'm serious about this, about her."

"For all I know, it's just an expensive prop."

Temper stirred and Myles lost some of the calm. "That ring is a family heirloom and not something I'd give to someone I didn't want or expect to keep as my wife."

Again with the speechlessness. Tucker's expression shifted to a consideration that made Myles hope he never faced the man from the witness stand.

"I hope that's true. I hope the whole thing

works out for both of you. Because if I find out that you've done this purely as a means of accessing that trust, I'm going to break you in half."

Myles shot him a humorless smile. "I suppose this is a bad time to ask you to be my best man."

Tucker blinked at him. "Are you serious?"

"You're one of the best friends I've made since I moved here, and I know it would mean a lot to Piper to have you stand up there with us."

Tucker laced his hands behind his head and paced away. "Way to make me feel like an asshole."

"Same goes. But you're looking out for Piper. I'm not going to be offended by that—much—since I'd do the same damned thing in your position."

"I don't know what to say."

"Look. I know this is completely insane. We both know that's Piper's specialty. But if it reassures you at all, I'm absolutely crazy about her. Have been from the moment I auditioned with her. And I swear to you I will do everything in my power not to fuck this up. The last thing I'd ever want to do is hurt her. Besides, being best man will give you a front row seat and opportunity to kick my ass if you think I'm out of line."

He laughed. "Then I guess I'm getting fitted for a tux."

"There's one more thing I need your help with."

"What's that?" Tucker asked warily.

"This wedding…the way my grandmother is planning it, the whole big public spectacle isn't what Piper wants. I can't do much to change that. But with your help, I can at least do something to make the whole thing a little more…Piper."

"What'd you have in mind?"

Myles outlined the plan that had been kicking around his brain all afternoon. "The deadline is insane, but if we can pull it off…"

Tucker clapped a hand on his shoulder. "Brother, that does more to put me at ease than anything else you've said. Everybody will be delighted to help. You just leave everything to me."

"WHERE'S YOUR MOM?" Tyler asked.

Piper clenched her jaw and shoved open the door to Brides and Belles. "Not coming."

Norah hurried after her. "Why? What happened?"

"We got into an argument at breakfast. Her feelings got hurt and now she's in a snit. Why the fact that I do not give a rat's ass what color the table cloths are justifies hurt feelings or a snit, I cannot explain, but I do not have the time or patience to talk her down, so we're dress shopping without her." Piper fixed a smile she absolutely didn't feel on her face as she stepped up to greet the store's owner. "Hi, Mrs. Wofford."

"You look like you could use one of our mimosas. I've already got a bottle of champagne chilling back in the dressing room."

"Oh my God, that sounds amazing."

"Did you remember your underthings?"

For a moment Piper balked. Of course, she'd put on underwear this morning. Then she realized Mrs. Wofford meant a strapless bra and Spanks. "I didn't. Kinda didn't think about that."

"I did," Norah announced.

"Of course, you did. Because you are all knowing and awesome. Thanks."

"You just head on back and get undressed. Fitting room one. I've already got a few dresses laid out for you to try."

"Thanks, Mrs. Wofford. I appreciate you fitting me in so last minute."

"Oh please, darlin', call me Babette."

Norah and Tyler followed Piper to the back.

"Miranda got called in at the hospital, so she won't be able to make it," Norah said.

"I'm on drink duty." Tyler went to work pouring mimosas as Piper went in and pulled the curtain. "So, what was the fight really about?"

"Underneath it all, the same old crap. She's offended by me being me. God forbid I get to do that for my own wedding."

Norah thrust the strapless bra past the curtain. "Did she miss the memo that you're awesome?"

"Awesome does not have the same definition in the world of Twyla Parish as it does for us. I am the black sheep daughter. I've always been the black sheep daughter. Leah's the one who did everything Mom wanted, cared about all the same things, got married right out of school and gave her an adorable grandbaby. Me, I can't do anything right."

"That's really not fair, Piper." Leah's voice was thick with hurt outside the dressing room.

Naturally she'd shown up in time to over-hear that.

Because she needed something to do with her hands, Piper unzipped the dress that seemed the least complicated and began to shimmy into it. "I've never thought it was fair. I'm a completely different person from both of you and nothing I've ever done has seemed to be enough to earn your approval. Almost all my life it's been 'Why can't you be more like Leah?' And now I'm getting married and suddenly you're both all smiles and happy because I finally did something right. I'm sorry if I resent the hell out of that." She threw back the curtain and stalked out, one arm holding the dress across her breasts. "Somebody zip me, please."

Norah hurried to comply.

Leah's cheeks flushed pink. "We're happy for you and you're going to criticize us for that?"

Piper closed her eyes and counted to ten. She didn't want to fight with her sister. She didn't want to fight with anyone. "That isn't what I'm saying." Blowing out a breath, she accepted the mimosa Tyler held out and downed half of it. "I appreciate the fact that you're both happy for me and that you've thrown yourself into the cause to help pull together this wedding last minute. I really do."

At Babette's urging, she stepped up onto the platform in front of the three-way mirror. The dress had an empire waist, with an explosion of beading on the bodice and a simple drape all the way to the floor.

"No," Norah and Tyler chorused.

Piper turned away from the mirror.

"Then what's the problem?" Leah asked.

"None of this is what I want."

Everybody went stock still, like deer in the headlights.

"Um."

Piper's gaze shot to the doorway, where Skye stood, mouth hanging open. Augusta stood just behind her.

Perfect. Just perfect. She'd insulted her future mother-in-law's husband just two days ago and now Augusta was going to think she was backing out of the wedding.

Piper downed the other half of the mimosa. "That isn't what I meant." She handed Tyler the glass and stepped off the platform to head for her future in-laws. "I want to marry Myles. I want to marry him next weekend. That isn't in question. It's just that..." She trailed off, not sure what she could say that wouldn't make her sound like an ungrateful bitch.

"My mother-in-law has come in and taken over?" Augusta suggested gently.

Piper exhaled in relief. "Yes. And my mom has jumped right on the band wagon."

"I'm afraid Suzanne has a habit of doing that."

"Have you seen the itineraries she's given us? This wedding has absolutely nothing to do with Myles and me personally. We might as well be living Ken and Barbie dolls up there for other people's entertainment."

"Why agree to it at all?"

"Because I felt like I needed to play nice to pacify everybody in the wake of that whole ugly scene when they found out we were getting married in the first place. My mom was offended—by my behavior, not hers, mind you—and I'm pretty sure I made the worst possible impression on Mrs. Stewart."

Augusta winced. "I expect her behavior made the worst possible impression on you. Let me apologize for that again and assure you that there's no need to pacify anyone."

"Water under the bridge." God knew there was no reason to stay upset about it when nothing could be done to change it.

"For what it's worth, she admires your moxie. So do I."

It was Piper's turn to wince. "Is that a nice way of saying you're not mad at me for calling out Myles' dad?"

"Warrick is...set in his ways and has never quite gotten over the fact that Myles has a different path. Someone needed to say it. That it was someone not part of our family had more impact than anything Myles has said over the years. So no, I'm not at all angry. I appreciate your defense of my son."

"Uh, Piper, you might want to continue this conversation on the other side of the curtain. You're on a tight schedule," Norah reminded her.

"Oh, we don't want to intrude," Augusta began.

"Speak for yourself. I want to get to know my new sister-in-law." Skye flounced in and plopped onto one of the dainty sofas.

Augusta wasn't nearly so comfortable. "Myles mentioned you'd be here this morning, and we thought we might stop in."

Piper reached out to squeeze one of her hands, grateful for her show of support. "Please stay. I'd like to get to know you better, too."

As Babette unzipped her, Piper made quick introductions. Then she stepped behind the curtain, stripping out of the first dress and working her way into the next.

"Can we get in on those mimosas?" Skye asked.

"Coming right up," Tyler said.

Piper heard the pouring of more drinks. "I want another, too."

"So why not just tell Gram what you want?" Skye asked.

"Because when I agreed to this, I honestly didn't think I cared. I was never one of those girls who spent a lot of time fantasizing about my wedding. What was two weeks of crazy when the end result meant I'd be married to Myles either way?"

Babette zipped her up and made a few adjustments.

She stepped out of the dressing room and in front of the mirrors. "Plus, I honestly didn't think she could pull together anything so elaborate in so short a time. Clearly, I was wrong."

This dress was a classic princess style, with a sweetheart neckline and miles of tulle making the skirt flare out like a bell.

"Oh, that's beautiful," Leah gushed. Apparently, she'd decided to let go of her snit for now.

She would like this dress. It strongly resembled the one she'd worn for her wedding.

"Too floofy," Tyler declared.

"It's not you," Norah decided.

Piper retreated back to the dressing room.

"What exactly did you want out of a wedding?" Skye asked.

"I wanted to elope and miss the circus entirely. Just him and me and the minister on the beach. Barefoot. Some kind of unconventional, tropical flowers in a loose bouquet. My hair down. Or maybe a partial up-do to keep it out of my face with the wind."

"What if you did something more vintage?" Tyler suggested. "Do your hair like you did for the show last fall. Wear something with that kind of forties glam style, like the dress you wore for the scene in The Carousel Club. You were a knockout in that."

Piper sipped at her mimosa and considered. "That's a possibility. Myles loved that dress."

"I remember. He practically drooled all through that scene from dress rehearsal through closing night."

"Hmmm. Wait right here. I think I have something that might suit." Babette slipped past the curtain. She came back a few minutes later with another dress in ivory satin. "Let's try this one."

Piper shimmied into the dress, waiting patiently as she was laced in and adjusted.

"Okay, nobody say anything this time. I want Piper to see this one with no other feedback first," Babette ordered.

Piper shuffled out, which was about the best she could manage in the tight skirt.

Babette gave her a hand up on the stage. "Close your eyes."

She did as ordered, letting the older woman pull her into place. "Okay, now, open."

"Oh." It was the only thing Piper could manage.

This dress also had a sweetheart neckline, but whereas the last one had swallowed her, this one hugged her curves from breast to knee before flaring out in a chapel length mermaid style skirt. The entire thing was ruched, from the lace applique bodice down.

This was the dress.

I'm getting married. Despite all the hoopla

that'd been going on the last week, all the plans, all the details, nothing had brought home the reality like standing here in this dress that seemed made just for her. She'd walk down the aisle to Myles in this and watch his eyes darken with wanting. And maybe something more.

Piper realized she'd reached out to touch two fingers to her image in the mirror. "I'm getting married in this dress."

"It's perfect," Norah said.

"You're gorgeous," Tyler assured her.

Leah stepped up on the stage and laid a light hand on her back. "It's you. It's so absolutely you."

Piper turned to hug her. "I'm sorry I was pissy."

"I'm sorry we were pushy."

As Norah and Tyler helped her up off the little stage, Piper laughed. "Good thing we aren't doing a church wedding. I don't think I could manage stairs in this."

"You know, since number three was the charm, and it doesn't look like it's going to require any alterations, that means we are officially ahead of schedule," Norah said.

"And?" Piper asked.

"And I called ahead to the Babylon. They've got two hours of spa treatments lined up for all six of us—Augusta and Skye included."

"Did I mention I love you?"

Norah grinned. "I do what I can."

"PRESTON, BABY, YOU JUST have to walk from daddy down here to me, okay?" Leah's pleading fell on deaf ears.

As their cranky ring bearer screwed up his face and began to bawl, Myles was wishing *he* was deaf.

Piper's sister cringed in mortification, holding her son by his little shoulders. "Sweetheart, there's no need for all that."

Big, fat tears rolled down his reddened face and his wail echoed off the nearby buildings. Gram heaved a long-suffering sigh. They'd been trying to coax him down the aisle for fifteen minutes.

Looking embarrassed himself, Elliott started apologizing. "I'll just take him down."

Myles broke from his position beneath the pergola and headed toward the chaos. "Let me try." He crouched down in front of his soon-to-be nephew. "Hey, little man."

The wailing cut off, even though the tears kept rolling.

"It's awful confusing up here, isn't it, with all these people? Are you not wanting to leave your Aunt Pie?"

"Pie?" Preston sniffed hopefully, looking up at Piper.

"See, here's how this is supposed to work. Everybody's gonna be marching down this aisle here toward the front. Miss Norah, Miss Miranda, and Miss Tyler come down. Then you get to lead Aunt Pie down carrying this pillow here." He stuck out a hand and took it from Elliott.

"Pie."

"That's right. If you can come all the way down like a big boy and stand with me, I'll boost you up on my shoulders so you can see her coming over everybody else."

"Oh, I don't—"

Myles cut Leah off with his hand. "Would you like that?"

Preston nodded slowly.

"Okay then." Myles swiped at the tears on his baby soft cheeks, feeling a curious pull. "We cool?"

The kid offered up his fist. Grinning, Myles bumped it. "Good job. Now I'm gonna be right down front. You just have to come to me."

"My!"

"That's right." Myles trotted back to his place beside the minister. "Let's try that again."

The processional started. The attendants, predictably, made it down the aisle. Then it was time for Preston. With one last look at his aunt, he trotted the length of the aisle, albeit at about twice the tempo of the song. But he made it, coming straight to Myles.

"Great job, buddy!" He gave the boy another fist bump, then lifted him up on his shoulders to watch the rest of the show.

Preston immediately grabbed his ears, as if they were reins, leaning forward to look for his aunt. "Pie?"

"She's coming. Just watch."

She'd opted not to be escorted and flounced down the aisle with a bow bouquet and a silly face for her nephew that was clearly trying Gram's tolerance for lack of decorum. Preston bounced, clapping his hands against Myles' head. Myles shifted his grip on the kid to make sure he didn't slide down in his excitement.

Tucker leaned in. "Your grandmother doesn't look thrilled with the deviation from the plan," he murmured.

"Nope."

"She's really going to have a fit over what you've really planned for tomorrow."

"Yep."

"You really want to go through with it?"

Myles thought of the surprise he'd roped

their theater friends into for Piper. They'd been working feverishly all week to pull it off. "At the end of the day it's our wedding. Gram wants a production. We'll give her one."

Piper took her place beside him beneath the vine covered pergola. "Good job, Pres."

"MyPie!" he cheered.

"That's it," Myles said. "We're legit now. We've officially been made a portmanteau."

Piper grinned. "Well, I supposed it's better than Myper or Piles."

"Dearly beloved. Uh, Myles, would you like to divest yourself of your passenger?" Reverend Emmons asked.

"Nah, I'm good. He's happy. The sooner we get through this, the sooner we can all go eat."

That ended up being an excellent tactic. They were able to zip through the steps of the ceremony in twenty minutes, with one more trial run of the processional for Preston to walk down to Myles and wait for Piper—from the ground this time.

"And then you'll all recess in reverse order

and make your way to the elevator and down to the top floor to wait, while guests clear out to the reception in the ballroom before coming back up here for pictures."

"By jove, I think we've got it," Myles declared. "And I think we're all starving. You hungry, little man?"

"Yeah!"

"Me too!" Myles handed him off to Leah, who shook her head in amazement.

"Piper may have competition for favorite relative. You're great with him."

"I get a kick out of him." Way more than he'd expected. Myles had never been around small children that much. All his friends from his big city paper days were focused on career, as he'd been. Few of them were married and none of them had been thinking about families. Watching Leah walk away with a waving Preston perched on her hip, he thought they were probably missing out.

At the head of the aisle, Piper leaned in to give her nephew a smacking kiss, making the little boy giggle with delight. She was so re-laxed and easy with kids. It was easy to imagine her beaming at another little face with her impish grin and his eyes. She'd make a great mom, and it'd be fun to see what kind of trouble their little black sheep family could get into.

Family.

Well, holy shit.

Piper slipped her arm through his. "You re-alize you've just been drafted for the official babysitting roster, right?"

Still reeling from his little fantasy, he mur-mured, "I don't mind. It's good practice." He didn't realize that had slipped out of his mouth until he saw the stunned expression on Piper's face. "You know, for someday."

"Someday," she echoed.

Add that to the list of things we really ought to discuss.

It hadn't seemed pertinent in the beginning, when this had been more of a favor with a the-oretical expiration date. But with each passing day, he was realizing he didn't want an expiration date. He wanted to do this for real.

He held out his hand. "Rehearsal dinner?"

She slipped her hand in his. "Rehearsal dinner."

THE REHEARSAL DINNER slipped by without incident—a minor miracle as far as Piper was concerned. Given how fast this whole shindig had been thrown together, she kept expecting some disaster to strike that would cause Myles' grandmother to permanently curse their names. Sooner than she expected, her girlfriends were dragging her away from her groom in the name of bachelorette party.

Piper felt strangely nervous about letting him go. He'd been uncharacteristically quiet all through dinner, and she worried he was having second thoughts.

"You'll see him tomorrow," Miranda insisted.

Piper ignored her, slipping her arms around Myles and searching his face. "You sure you're okay?"

"My toes are perfectly toasty," he assured her. "This time tomorrow, all the crazy will be over and we'll be celebrating. Go have fun with the girls." He sent an arch look in their direction. "No strippers, y'all."

Tyler crossed her heart. "No strippers. We've got something else in mind."

Myles brushed a thumb across her cheek, much as he'd done to Preston earlier. The gesture made her heart roll over in her chest.

"See you tomorrow, Mrs. Stewart."

"Tomorrow," she sighed.

Tyler and Norah had her shoved into a car before she could so much as blink.

"Where are we going?" Piper demanded.

"You, my darling, need to loosen up. You're getting married tomorrow," Tyler announced.

"I did remember that, believe it or not."

"That's why you need loosening up," Miranda said.

"I will loosen up once we are on the other side of the 'I do's and Suzanne and her entourage have left town."

"This will help." Norah passed a gift bag from the front seat. "Go ahead and open it."

Piper pulled tissue paper out and stuck her hand inside, fingers wrapping around something long and textured. Mildly afraid of what X-rated thing they'd concocted, she slowly pulled the thing from the bag—and began to laugh hysterically. Deep belly spasms of mirth.

"A bedazzled microphone?"

"We're doing bachelorette karaoke," Tyler declared. "Because *of course*. It's you."

Piper felt some of the tension that'd been lodged in her chest all week loosen. "Have I mentioned I love y'all?"

"We never get tired of hearing it," Miranda said, swinging an arm around her shoulders.

Karaoke night had always been a bimonthly event at Speakeasy. But it was only in the wake of the hugely successful community theater fundraiser back in the fall—brainchild of Myles and Tucker—that it'd become a seriously popular local event. No surprise, to Piper's mind. You put all the most talented local singers on stage and people tended to enjoy it more than total caterwauling. Ever since, the theater crowd had made a monthly pilgrimage to binge on pizza and sing. Partly to keep in practice and partly because it was just fun. There was rarely more than one musical per season at The Madrigal Theater.

Tonight wasn't theater night. But when Piper and her friends stepped into Speakeasy, at least half the people present were part of that crowd. At the sight of her, a cheer went up, followed by applause and shouts of congratulations.

"The bride-to-be has arrived. We can officially declare this bachelorette version of karaoke night open!" Joby Tisdale announced.

Hoots and hollers followed this declaration.

"Piper, would you like to kick us off?" he asked.

"Sure." She made her way through the room,

shaking hands and accepting hugs on her way to flip through the book of songs that she knew almost by heart.

What says I'm getting married tomorrow?

She had Joby cue up Meghan Trainor's "Dear Future Husband" and worked to put on some sass for the number. Her girls lined up behind her for backup, adding impromptu fifties style choreography, while she sang and simpered to the audience. But she just…wasn't feeling her usual zing. If the audience noticed, they certainly gave no indication. The applause made her miss Myles. She'd gotten used to singing with him here. Flirting through song had been the most fun she'd had in ages. Being with Myles in general was fun. He delighted in saying and doing the outrageous, just to make her smile. Which made them exceedingly well matched.

She just wished he were here with her tonight.

Oh for heaven's sake, woman, you'll see him tomorrow. You're marrying him tomorrow.

She waited for some kind of nerves to hit as Tyler took the little stage for a rendition of "Exes and Ohs." And though she felt some unease, it had nothing to do with Myles and everything to do with the grand social event his grandmother had planned. Much as she enjoyed performing, she didn't want to be on display for her actual personal life. A part of her worried that they wouldn't survive all the scrutiny.

She wanted a chance for them to focus just on them. No audience. No pressure. No loan repayment hanging over their heads. Just her and Myles. As things would have been had his investor not decided to pull out.

Just one more day. Then the circus will be over.

But because she was missing him, Piper put herself back in the queue with Gershwin's "Someone To Watch Over Me."

They'd made their order for an extra-large sausage and mushroom pie and garlic knots by the time her turn rolled around again. Piper took the stage and began to sing. She poured all the longing she felt into the music, automatically making it a true performance, not just a song. The door opened and, as if she'd summoned him with the power of her voice, Myles stepped inside, followed by Tucker and Brody.

Nobody was looking at him. But she felt it the moment his eyes met hers. His lips curved, slow and sexy, and he crossed the restaurant toward the stage, taking an empty seat. Piper took her bedazzled microphone and left the stage, singing to him now as she wound her way through the crowd and sat on his lap for the final few bars of the song.

Everybody went nuts.

She flipped off the mic and leaned in to kiss him. His hand snaked up her back and into her hair as he slanted his head to take the kiss deeper. Winding her arms around his shoulders, she relaxed in to that strange mix of comfort and heat. How could he make her feel so safe and reckless in the same moment?

"Hey!" Miranda protested. "This is a bachelorette party. You can't be here."

In response, Myles slid his arms around Piper's waist, holding her in place. "I do believe it is a free country. And we men wanted to sing."

"I think you knew I was missing you," Piper whispered, nuzzling into his shoulder.

"I was missing you back," he murmured.

"Objection!" Tucker declared. "You're not supposed to hang out with your intended the night before the wedding."

"Piper and I haven't done a damn thing the traditional way in the course of our relationship. Why on Earth would we start now? That wouldn't suit her or me. We stay. Get on the roster."

"You, me, 'Wanted, Dead or Alive'," Brody announced, heading for the list.

Piper stared at Myles.

"What?" he asked.

"You really get me."

"I should hope so. I've made rather a study of it."

An ache set up in her chest and she pushed up, suddenly needing to move, needing space.

"What's wrong?"

"Nothing." She squeezed his hand. "I just need a breath of air. I'll be back in a minute."

"I'll come with you."

He started to rise, but she just pushed him back into his seat, smiling. "You and Brody are up next. Don't want to miss your cue. Really, I'll be right back."

Weaving through the tables, she headed for the door. Her skin felt flushed and freezing at once and her heart was beating a rat-a-tat-tat in her chest that was more akin to terror than exhilaration.

The cool night air helped a little. The bands around her chest loosened a fraction. But not the ache somewhere in the vicinity of her heart. That still throbbed like a bad tooth. Absently, she rubbed at it.

"You okay?" Tucker's voice came from behind.

"I'm fine." Total lie.

He circled around to look her in the face. "This is me you're talking to. How are you really?"

Her breath gushed out. "Terrified. It's like stage fright times a thousand."

A muscle jumped in Tucker's jaw as he looked out over the green. "Myles told me what you're doing."

Piper's gaze snapped to his. "I thought maybe you'd figured it out."

"Well, what I thought was a lot less flattering. I accused him of using you."

"Tucker!"

"I should've known better. It's so very you to make that kind of major, snap decision. But you don't have to do this. This is real life, not a play. He'll understand if you back out."

Myles had been giving her chances to back out for two weeks. She knew him well enough to be certain that if she bailed, he'd be more concerned about her than about the impact her decision would have on his business. Which was why she knew she was going through with it.

"I'm not nervous because I think I'm making a mistake, Tucker. I'm nervous because I'm in love with Myles." If she expected the admission to quell the panic, she was sadly mistaken.

"I'd think that'd be the preferred state you'd want to be in since you're marrying the guy."

Piper wrapped both arms around her middle. "I wasn't when we started this. Not completely. And I don't know if he's there yet or not. I know he cares about me. I know he's attracted to me. But I don't know if he feels what I feel, and I'm afraid that we'll go through with this and something will go horribly wrong. All other things being equal, I think there's a big chance we'd have ended up here anyway, and I'm terrified that this crazy plan of ours will screw that up somehow."

"Love's a risk, even under more conventional circumstances. But I think you stand a great shot at making it. I've watched you two together all week. You've got each other's back.

If this doesn't work out, I don't think it'll be because one of you feels less than the other."

"You really think so?"

"The guy's crazy about you. If he's not in love with you yet, he's only about half a step away."

Piper narrowed her eyes at him. "You say that like you know something I don't know."

Tucker held up his hands. "I'm just calling it like I see it. I do have eyes, last I checked."

Was that what other people saw when they looked at her and Myles?

"Do you know why absolutely nobody questioned the story you told when you announced the engagement?" he asked.

She shook her head.

"Because it was completely believable. And I'd have bought it myself if I hadn't had inside information. The bigger surprise wasn't the announcement. It's that you actually *weren't* together all those months. You two fit."

"I'm the only reason we weren't. Together, I mean."

"Yeah, yeah. The rule. I always thought that rule was kinda dumb."

"You never fell for your co-star because of the role, instead of who *they* were."

"Did it ever occur to you that what happened with Brandon was just a relationship naturally fizzling out once the infatuation was finished?"

"Yes. That's why I had the rule. I figured if the infatuation lasted, if he waited for me, then there was something more substantial there. Myles waited. No question, no pressure, just respect for my decision, even though he knew perfectly well that it wouldn't have taken much to make me change my mind."

"He's a good guy," Tucker conceded.

"One of the best I've known. And he's going to start worrying if I don't get back in there."

Tucker stood and offered his hand. "Okay then. Let's go sing your last single hours away."

"YOU'RE MARRYING ONE OF my best friends today."

Myles caught sight of Tucker's grave expression in the mirror's reflection. They were alone in the groom's suite, the other groomsmen having gone off to do more of Gram's bidding. The ceremony was scheduled to start in less than half an hour. Praying for patience, he turned toward his best man, bracing himself for a repeat of the scene they'd had at The Mudcat. They really didn't have time for this.

"I know."

"I've still got my reservations about the wisdom of this whole thing, but I do believe you legitimately care about her and that you're not going to fuck it up on purpose."

Myles offered a wry smile. "Thanks. I think."

"I just wanted you to know that I'm with you, when I'm standing up there. As a friend, not a potential bouncer."

Something in Myles' chest eased. "Thanks, Tuck. That means a lot."

Tucker swung an arm around his shoulders. "How's your voice? Warmed up?"

Myles sang a few scales. He was on key but his voice was shaking. Well, he figured he was entitled.

"Nervous?"

"About marrying Piper, not at all. About this bait and switch we're pulling without having a true rehearsal…"

"You just worry about you and your piece. We've got the rest. And remember, it's just like being in a show."

"Except in a show I can't actually see the audience for the stage lights."

"I've seen Piper. Trust me, once you see her, you won't be able to see anything else."

"What if she hates the surprise?"

"She won't," Tucker assured him. "She's going to love every minute of it. The fact that you thought of it shows how well you understand her. And that you organized it and made it happen proves how much you care. Just breathe. In a little over thirty minutes, the hard part will be over."

Brody barged back into the suite. "They're seating guests already. It's gonna be a full house. Or roof, as it were. Probably standing room only. But don't worry. All our people will be in place before the ceremony begins. Everybody's warmed up and ready to go." He narrowed his eyes at Myles. "Are *you?* You're looking a little sweaty."

"I'm good. I'm just ready to get this over with and get to the party with my wife."

Brody slapped him on the back. "Look at

you saying 'wife' like it ain't no thing. You got this."

"Give it a few months. You'll be right behind."

"Damn skippy. Can't wait," Brody said.

Another knock came on the door. "Are you decent?" A moment later Myles' mother stepped into the room.

"What are you doing down here? Shouldn't you be upstairs getting ready for the seating of the parents?" he asked.

"Yes, and you need to be on the roof in ten minutes yourself. But it's not like they can start without you."

Ten minutes. Jesus. That meant about fifteen minutes until he blew his grandmother's mind in an effort to surprise his bride.

Myles shoved both hands through his hair.

"Can I have a minute alone with my son?"

"Sure thing. See you up there, buddy." Tucker headed out, followed by Brody.

Augusta reached out and smoothed her

hands along his shoulders and down his lapels. "You look so handsome in your tux."

"I suppose I clean up pretty well. Was there something you wanted to tell me, Mom?"

"I just wanted to see my baby one last time before he got married." She squeezed his hands. "I'm really proud of you, Myles. I'm proud of the fact that you fought for your dream. I know you haven't heard that enough from us, and I'm sorry for that. The fact is, you've grown into such an amazing man. And I'm so pleased that you've found an equally amazing woman who believes in you so completely. Piper's lovely and she'll be a good partner for you. That's so important in a marriage."

What would she say if she knew they'd been together only two weeks?

"Piper is...one of a kind. She's got the biggest heart of anyone I know, and I can only hope to one day really deserve her."

Augusta frowned. But before she could say anything else, Skye stuck her head in the door.

"It's time!"

Myles exhaled a slow breath. *Show time.*

He escorted his mom and sister to the elevator. "I need to move. I'm gonna take the stairs."

On his way down the hall, the door to the bride's suite started to open. Miranda peered out. "Nope! Coast is not clear! Keep her back."

"I'm going, I'm going." Breaking into a trot, he made for the stairwell, letting the door slap shut behind him. For a moment, he just stood in the cool concrete tower. Then he climbed the last flight to the roof.

Holy shit.

When Brody had said standing room only, he wasn't kidding. The hanging gardens inspired by the hotel's namesake were packed with guests. Myles felt his heart kick, his pulse a driving timpani beat in his ears. How was he even going to hear the music?

Tucker broke from where he stood at the periphery, waiting to head up to the altar.

"Breathe," he ordered. "None of these people are important. They're just props."

"Props," Myles repeated. He sucked in a few ragged breaths, then nodded. "Props."

They headed up front together. Brody and Grady were waiting.

His brother offered a hand. "Congratulations, big brother. You've clearly got better taste in women than I do."

"Goes without saying." But Myles softened the words with a smile. "Thanks."

Margot, the events coordinator for The Babylon, said something into a headset. She gave a hand signal and whatever music Gram had picked for the seating of the grandmothers and parents began to play. She'd had a bit of a fit that it was recorded rather than a live string quartet, but they'd needed the space for guest seating. Myles was too nervous to actually listen to it. This was the last part of Gram's plan that would go entirely to script.

Gram looked beautiful and stately in a pale blue suit, her snow-white hair catching the rays of the setting sun as she strolled, ruler-straight down the aisle. Piper's grandmothers, whom he'd met very briefly at the rehearsal dinner, followed. Then came his mother. Then Twyla. Then the song ended.

When another didn't immediately begin, Myles saw Margot hiss something into the headset. Whatever answer came back absolutely flummoxed her, and he couldn't help but smile. To his left, he heard the clear tone of Tucker's pitch pipe.

In the audience, Gram's attention shot to Tucker with a murderous glare. All around her, audience members shifted and straightened, waiting for the prearranged signal.

Oh man, she was gonna hate this.

Myles grinned and the first clear voices rang out in acapella harmony. He added his own on the bass line and waited for the doors to open.

"It's time. They're nearly finished with the seating of the mothers," Norah reported. "Are you ready?"

Piper pressed a hand to her belly, where a flock of seagulls was trying to beat its way out. This whole thing had been a lot less terrifying before she'd realized she was in love with Myles. The prospect of being great friends with spousal benefits had seemed like a fantastic idea. But they'd both been on an even playing field then.

Loving him and not knowing if he'd ever feel the same made the risk she took so much greater.

She tried to hold on to Tucker's words from the night before. *The guy's crazy about you. If he's not in love with you yet, he's only about half a step away.*

She hoped and prayed that Tucker was right.

You just have to believe he'll get there.

Blowing out a breath, she straightened and took her bouquet from Tyler. "Let's do this."

She stepped into the elevator with her attendants. The ride to the roof was hardly long enough to take a breath. They spilled out of the elevator and into the vestibule to line up. Elliott held Preston to keep him from running out. Tucker and Tyler had the actual rings, just in case he flipped out and didn't make it down the aisle. Everything was in place. A couple of hotel employees stood prepared to open the double doors to the outside.

Piper crossed to Preston, running a hand down his little vest. "Aren't you a handsome boy in your fancy duds."

He flashed a toothy grin.

"You remember how we practiced last night? You're going to wait until Norah, Miranda, and Tyler go. Then you'll go from me to Uncle Myles, down front. Okay?"

Preston clapped. "MyPie!"

"That's right. This is all about MyPie." She kissed his little nose and made him giggle. Turning to her friends, she gave each of them a last hug in turn. "Thank y'all for being here. It means a lot to me." More than she'd realized it would.

"We wouldn't have missed it for the world,"

Tyler said.

And suddenly, Piper was glad of the wedding, glad to have her friends and family here. Even if nothing else about this day had been designed with her in mind, she'd have this memory with them.

She watched them line up, clutching their own bouquets.

"Ready, ma'am?" one of the hotel staff asked.

"As I'll ever be."

The woman spoke into a headset. After a few moments' hesitation, they opened the doors.

Piper frowned, hearing…voices, not strings. "This isn't Pachelbel."

From the rear of the line, Tyler looked over and grinned. "Yeah, about that. Myles arranged for us to hijack the music. You're welcome." Then she turned forward and began to belt out the introduction to "Seasons of Love" from the musical RENT as Norah started bopping her way down the aisle in all her rhythmically challenged glory.

Piper peeked around the edge of the door. At least a quarter of the audience was on their feet, singing and swaying in place. She recognized almost everyone she'd ever performed with. Her chest clenched and she covered her mouth to hold in something between laughter and tears. From the front, Myles' voice rang out in harmony with Tucker and Brody as they hit the chorus.

He'd arranged for a flash mob at their wedding.

Oh my God, I love this man.

She could just barely see him as Miranda made her way down during the second verse, his shoulders twitching in time to the music. Beside him, Tucker and Brody grinned like a couple of court jesters as they continued to sing. At the far end, Grady stood stiff as a board, eyes wide, as if he'd just realized his brother had been body snatched. Piper sincerely hoped Myles' grandmother didn't have a heart condition.

Tyler pivoted into place at the front, just in

time for a solo, by which time most of the audience was swaying along with the performers. Piper didn't even realize Preston was dancing his way to the front until he was halfway down the aisle. She repressed a laugh. At least he was headed in the right direction. He went straight to Myles and earned a fist bump for his trouble before Leah snagged him.

When they finished, silence hung heavy over the crowd. She saw a few people pause with their hands hovering inches apart, uncertain whether to applaud. So she let out a two finger whistle and clapped herself to get them going.

As the applause faded, her pulse kicked up, waiting to see what she was, in fact, walking down the aisle to. A murmur ran through the guests as Myles stepped out of the lineup and moved to the head of the aisle so he faced her directly. His face was a shade or two paler than normal, and sweat beaded his brow.

Oh no. Was he going to bolt from the altar?

Somebody blew a note on a pitch pipe. The

performers set up a soft acapella accompaniment. Myles took a breath and began to sing.

Oh. Oh God.

She couldn't move. Couldn't do anything but stare at him with her heart cracked open wide as he serenaded her with "Take Me As I Am" from *Jekyll and Hyde.*

His voice floated over the audience, twining around her heart as he sang to her and her alone. Everything in the music, in his eyes told her, *You see me. The real me. Here I am. I'm yours.* Of all the songs he could've chosen, none could have meant more from one black sheep to another. Wasn't that his biggest appeal? That he saw her, the real her, and accepted her without reservation? Wasn't that what they brought to each other?

As he reached the end of his verse, her nerves melted away and she took her first measured step toward him, wishing like hell her dress wasn't laced quite so tight as she launched into what might be the most important performance of her life. The guests faded away, and for the length of that aisle, there was nothing and no one but Myles. She poured out everything she felt. Making the promise that if he'd only look deep enough, he'd see that she loved him. The real him. Her voice gained strength with every step, until she joined voice and hands with him beneath the pergola as they sang vows of love and acceptance, no matter what.

Sliding a hand around her waist, he drew her in, lowering his brow to hers as they softly sang the final line. "Take me as I am."

The minister's voice broke the ensuing silence, reminding Piper that they weren't alone and the wedding wasn't over. "Well, that almost makes the vows seem superfluous."

She grinned over at him. "We should probably do them anyway."

"And so we shall. If there are no further surprises?" Reverend Emmons looked to Myles, then over to Tucker, who made an innocent face. Hearing no other interruptions, he continued. "Dearly beloved—"

CHAPTER 10

"**N**OT A DRY EYE in the house!"

Myles flinched as yet another camera flash went off in his periphery. "Zach, do you really have to keep doing that?"

"According to your grandmother, yes. And she's scarier than you."

"Of course she is," he muttered.

Piper chuckled. "You turned our wedding into a musical. This means there must be documentation and that it will be talked about for years to come."

He scowled. "I didn't do it for them. I did it for you."

She lifted her hands to frame his cheeks, pulling him close. "And I love that you did. You took the circus and made it about us. About me. I didn't really think that was possible. So thank you."

"You were getting little enough out of this whole deal."

Her expression as she smiled up at him made Myles' heart squeeze. "I got you out of it. That's all I wanted." Rising to her toes, she closed the last of the distance, pressing a soft kiss to his lips.

He heard the click of the camera again and lifted his head. "Zach, I swear to God... If you don't let me kiss my wife in peace, I'm going to kick your ass."

"But this stuff is gold. I'll have a seriously hard time picking the right shot for the front page of tomorrow's edition."

"If there is one word about this wedding in

tomorrow's edition, heads are going to roll," Myles snarled.

"But people love love! This will boost circulation."

"I'm not exploiting my personal life in the name of the paper. Now go away before I lose my good mood."

Zach wisely lowered the camera. "Fine, fine. I'll go find someone else to bug. But you can't control what ends up on Facebook and Instagram."

Eyes narrowed, Myles watched his friend weave his way through the crowded ballroom. "Remind me why we're still here?"

"Because we promised to play nice and we haven't discharged our duties as bride and groom."

"We danced. We ate dinner. We had cake. We even did the damned receiving line. What more do they want from us?"

"To hang out a respectable length of time before the bouquet toss."

"Define 'respectable.'"

"Long enough that they don't think we've snuck away from our own reception to have a quickie in the coat room."

And just like that, all the blood he'd been conscientiously trying to keep in his skull drained south. Myles pulled her closer to hide that reaction from the rest of the guests. "First, a quickie is a physical impossibility with you in that dress. I may require an engineering degree to get you out of it. Second, I am not going to make love to my wife for the first time in a coat closet. Third, I have every intention of taking my sweet time about it, which I'm eager to get started on, so really, how important is the stinking bouquet?"

Her eyes dilated and her breath quickened, which did marvelous things for the décolletage pressed against his chest. "I'm thinking we've been respectable enough."

"Well then, Mrs. Stewart, let's figure out our exit strategy."

Before they made it more than three yards, they were intercepted by his parents.

"Oh Myles, I just had no idea," his mother gushed.

That I've got a hard-on for my wife? Hand on Piper's waist, he shifted her subtly in front of him. "About what?"

"That you had that in you. I mean, you were good in *White Christmas*. But this—" She clasped her hands and looked between the two of them, her eyes getting teary. "It was just lovely. That must've taken so much rehearsal."

"I'm pretty wiped out. I didn't sleep much the last week," he admitted. *See there, I'm tired. We want to get out of here. Take the hint.*

"It was a great surprise," Piper said, leaning back into him.

Augusta's eyes widened. "You didn't know?"

"Nope. Just as surprised as the rest of you."

"But your performance was so perfect."

"The song is one of my favorites, and Myles and I sing together often."

Warrick shifted from foot-to-foot. Myles waited for his father to make some insulting remark. "It's unexpected," he finally managed.

Well, that was about as neutral a statement as he could make.

"I guess I've never been very accepting of the fact that you've always defied my expectations."

Piper stiffened, and Myles braced himself for some kind of confrontation.

"I'm sorry for that. You've made a good life for yourself, with a good wife, a good business. And maybe you haven't done any of it like I would have, but you've made it work. A lot of men couldn't manage that."

As apologies went, it was rather lukewarm, and judging by the pained look Warrick shot Augusta, his mother was the impetus behind it. But it was more than he'd ever offered before, so Myles wasn't about to look a gift horse in the mouth.

"Thanks, Dad."

"I wanted to give you something. A bit of a peace offering." Warrick reached into his coat pocket and drew out a thick envelope.

Automatically, Myles took it. "What is it?"

"A cruise. I know you don't have a lot of time just now, but it's a three-day trip to the Bahamas, leaving from Miami on Monday morning. It might end up being a little bit longer than you were planning to be gone, but your wife deserves your undivided attention."

"That's very kind of you, Mr. Stewart. Thank you."

He shifted his attention to Piper. "Young lady, you're a part of our family now. If you've got the *cojones* to call me out for my bad behavior, you can certainly call me by name."

Her shoulders shook with silent laugher. "Thank you, Warrick. We appreciate it."

"Thank you," Myles said. "Both of you. This wedding wouldn't have happened without your help. Or Gram."

"She's just happy to see you settled," Augusta said.

"Even if I did hijack her carefully planned ceremony?"

His mother waved that away. "She wanted something worthy of the society pages. You gave it to her in a way that no one is likely to top. Anyway, I expect you're both pretty exhausted. It's been a whirlwind couple of weeks."

On cue, Piper's jaw split with a yawn.

"Thought so. Let's find Margot. We'll get that bouquet toss done so you can get out of here."

Absolutely nobody was under the delusion that they were really tired, but Myles wasn't about to complain. He'd take whatever help he could get.

The ubiquitous Margot popped up as if they'd summoned her from a lamp. "Ready for your send off?"

"We are," Myles confirmed. "How exactly is that going to work since we're not actually leaving the hotel?"

"We're not?" Piper asked.

"I booked the honeymoon suite for the night."

She pivoted into him, tipping her lips toward his ear. "If I'd known that, I'd have dragged you off an hour ago."

Myles choked back a groan, his brain more than happy to provide ample inspiration for what they could've been doing for that hour.

"The suite is all ready, per your instructions. We'll just get the DJ to call together all the ladies for the toss, then everyone will line the ballroom to the lobby to see you to the elevator. Unless you have another preference?"

Having no better ideas, they gave their blessing. Leo Hamilton, one of Patty's sons and official DJ for the night, began blasting Beyonce's "Single Lady" over the PA. "Ladies, if you will gather on the dance floor, it's time for the bouquet toss!"

There was a rush of women to the center of the ballroom, his baby sister among them.

"What's Skye doing out there?"

"She's of age, big brother."

Myles scowled. "She is not. She should still be wearing pigtails."

"We'll have a discussion at a later date about how it's perfectly reasonable for her to be dating. I'm up." Picking up her skirts, Piper made her way to the front of the crowd. She looked around, focusing on Zach. "You ready?"

"Whenever you are," he called back.

Turning her back to the crowd, she waved the bouquet, once, twice, and on the third time hurled it into the air. The flowers sailed high, dropping down in the middle of the crowd. A scuffle broke out, and Myles could've sworn he heard a little shriek before a hand shot up, bouquet clutched in it. The other hopefuls fell away to reveal Simone, with her Cheshire cat grin dialed up to full wattage. From the sidelines, Omar gave her a thumb's up. Myles noted Mama Pearl giving her The Eye. He thought about passing on a warning to Simone—not just anyone would do for Mama Pearl's baby boy—but ultimately Myles decided he'd rather stay quiet and watch the fireworks as they happened. Besides, he had more important things to attend to right now.

Margot took the mic from Leo and began directing guests to line up for the send-off. Myles retrieved his bride, and they circled around to the end of the line. Zach took his place in front of them to catch the well-wishers throwing...wait, what the hell were they throwing? Surely not rice or bird seed inside?

Confetti. Silver and white confetti showered over the two of them as they hurried down the corridor of people. Wolf whistles and cheers chased them all the way into the lobby, where they made a beeline for the elevator a hotel employee was holding open.

Piper collapsed against the back wall, laughing as the doors closed. "I'm going to be picking confetti out of my hair and clothes for a week."

Myles swiped a hand over his tongue. "I'm pretty sure I ate some."

She heaved a relieved sigh. "Well, we did it. We survived the wedding. More importantly, we survived your grandmother. We—" She cut off, her face going slack with panic. "We forgot the prenup."

He hadn't even thought to have one drawn up after the two minutes of thought he'd given it the night she'd proposed. "I'm so not worried about the prenup."

"But I promised."

"You made a bigger promise on the roof." He gripped the railing on either side of her, effectively caging her with his body against the back wall. "So, unless you are having some ill-timed second thoughts, I believe that means we've arrived at the reward portion of the night."

Her hands splayed on his chest. "No second thoughts. Although since I didn't know we were going to be staying here tonight, I don't have any of my stuff here. I thought we'd swing by my place when we left."

"Yes, you do. I had Tyler pack you a bag."

Surprised pleasure flickered over her lovely face. "Do you think of everything, Mr. Stewart?"

"I try." The elevator dinged as they reached the top floor. Transferring his grip from the railing to her waist, he began backing out of the car. "Right now, though, all I can think about is you and me and the king-sized bed that's waiting down the hall."

"I support that plan," she said, a little breathless.

He bent and scooped her up.

On a giggle, she wrapped her arms around his shoulders. "Does it still count if the threshold you're carrying me over isn't home?"

"I'll do it there, too. Mostly I figure I can move faster carrying you than you can walk in this dress and those shoes."

"This is unarguable."

He carried her down the hall to their suite, having Piper dig the room key Margot had slipped him earlier in the day out of his breast pocket and sliding it into the lock. Then, kicking the door open, he carried his bride inside.

Moody jazz spilled out of the stereo speakers. Candles, not yet lit, were scattered around the room. Champagne iced in a bucket in one corner, and a room service cart with the cold supper that would keep until they got hungry again, was tucked in the breakfast nook. The double doors to the bedroom were thrown open to reveal the sprawling bed, scattered with rose petals.

He let Piper slide down his body, keeping hold of her even as her feet hit the floor.

Her eyes were wide, taking everything in. "I've never seen roses this color before."

"They're sterling silver."

"They're gorgeous. Is it to match the silver theme from the wedding?"

Myles looked into those warm, chocolate eyes. "They symbolize enchantment. Which seemed fitting, since you enchanted me from the moment I first met you. And now you're standing here with me as my wife." He couldn't keep the wonder out of his voice as he lifted her hands, pressing a kiss to the one that bore his rings.

Her lips curved. "You keep saying that."

"If I keep repeating it, maybe it'll start to feel real."

Piper slid her hands beneath his jacket,

shoving it off as she stepped close into him. "I've got a better idea for how we can do that."

His coat hit the floor with a soft whoosh of fabric that had Piper's pulse going thick with anticipation. She'd wanted him for months, almost from that first meeting at auditions. And now that wicked sense of humor and that poet's mouth were hers. No more waiting, no more reasons to hold back.

She worked the tie loose, using the length of it to drag his mouth just a hair's breadth from hers. "I do believe, Mr. Stewart, that you've been torturing me for days with the idea of claiming me as your wife. Time to pay up."

Heat flared in his eyes. But if she'd expected him to rush toward that finish line, she was disappointed.

"Oh, I fully intend to take my time about that." He brushed his mouth over hers in an unhurried kiss before stepping away.

Frustration shot through her. "A request, then."

"Anything within my power to grant," he promised, picking up a lighter and moving around the room, setting the candles alight.

"Once we get started, don't stop touching me."

"That is a promise I can absolutely keep." He set the lighter aside and moved to the suitcase.

"What are you doing?"

"Condoms. I want to make sure they're in easy reach."

"Not necessary. I'm on birth control. So unless you have some other objection…"

"Well, this night just gets better and better."

Holy hell, that hungry, predatory look on his face was a turn-on.

He seemed to scrape together some semblance of the civilized as he crossed back over to her, sliding his hands around her waist and drawing her to him. "I've been fantasizing about getting you out of this dress."

She was absolutely on board with that.

Naked was exactly where she wanted to be in short order. "Oh yeah? How does that fantasy go?"

"Something like this." He turned her so that he could get at the laces of the bodice. "Have I mentioned, I'm glad you left your hair down? So soft and lovely." He scooped it over one shoulder, running his fingers through the strands before applying his mouth to the sensitive skin of her neck, one hand flattened against her belly.

Piper felt her inner thighs loosen, wishing he'd take that hand either lower or higher. Or both. Without the barrier of the dress.

As if sensing her thoughts, he went to work on the laces, tugging them free of the loops, one by one, until the bodice loosened. "At first, I was annoyed by the laces because, talk about inefficient. But then I realized that it forces me to slow things down, build anticipation."

"I'm not sure I can take too much more anticipation."

She felt his smile against the bare skin of her shoulders.

"Oh, I think you can take quite a bit more, Mrs. Stewart." Those glorious, strong hands slid inside the dress to wrap around her torso, pulling her flush against him until she could feel his erection against her hip.

Impatient, Piper pressed back against him, satisfied at his groan. His palms slid up her body to cup her breasts. Her breath hissed out. Thank God the dress hadn't allowed for a bra. The cut and boning of the dress allowed just enough room for his hands to stroke and knead, pearling her nipples. There was something thrilling about being touched this way, intimate, but still mostly dressed.

"What happens next in this fantasy of yours?" she gasped, reaching back to grab his ass and pulling him more firmly against her.

"I get to play explorer."

"Explorer?"

"Mmm." Myles shifted, trailing one hand

lower, down the slope of her abs, until his fingers grazed the waistband of her panties.

Piper whimpered, wanting him to keep going, but the cut of the dress didn't leave room.

He tsked softly. "This will never do."

"Then you'd better take it off." *Please God, make it fast.*

He freed his hands, working the dress over her hips, until it puddled in the floor. She stepped out of it and her heels, using his hand for balance, until she stood before him in nothing but the lace thong and her pearls.

Myles' eyes went dark with desire, skimming down her body with stark appreciation. "God, you're so beautiful."

He spun her again, pulling her back against his chest and resuming his dual exploration, one hand loving her breasts, the other sliding beneath the waistband of her panties. As his hand dipped lower, fingers slipping between her folds, he sucked the shell of her ear into his mouth. Piper moaned, pressing into his palm, wanting, needing more of his touch. One finger slipped slowly inside her.

He lost some of his control, burying his face against her neck and holding her pinned against him. "God, you're so wet. This just got a thousand times better than my fantasy."

Her hips bucked, wanting so much more of him inside her. "More," she demanded.

"I did promise anything." He added a second finger to the first, stroking slowly in and out, spreading the moisture until his hand was drenched with it and she could barely stand.

"I think it's time we switched over to my fantasy," she gasped.

"I'm game. How does yours go?" He gave another curl of his fingers, rubbing over her clit with his thumb and making her clench around him.

"Mine involves a whole lot more naked. Get out of those clothes."

"As you wish." Between one blink and the next, he'd shed his shirt. Two more and he was naked. "Please tell me your fantasy involves my mouth on every inch of you."

Piper backed toward the bed. "Maybe with special attention to a few particular inches, south of the equator. Since you're in the mood to explore."

"Hell yes."

Before she could blink, Piper found herself bouncing back on the bed, with Myles prowling up her body like some kind of jungle cat. His hands slid up the outside of her thighs, fingers hooking in the waistband of the panties and working them down her legs until she was bare to him. He swore reverently, gripping her hips to hold her in place as he settled himself between her thighs.

The first touch of his tongue had her arching off the bed. He gave a slow, leisurely lick, as if learning her shape and taste.

"Mmm. You know what the best part of this is?"

"That I'm going to come in short order if

you get back to what you were doing?" she managed.

His lips curved against her. "Well, there's that. But no, the best part is that no other man will ever get this intimacy. No other man will ever know the taste of you, the scent of you. You're mine." This last he growled against her, and the vibrations sent a frisson of pleasure rippling through her. Then he set about proving that ownership, lapping and sucking until she was all but mindless with wanting. But not so mindless that she lost track of her own fantasy. As sensation built on sensation and her body strained toward release, Piper cried out. "Myles, stop. Stop!"

He froze, concern in his eyes. "What's wrong?"

She struggled to draw in enough breath to speak. "I want to come the first time with you inside me."

That predatory gleam flared in his eyes again, and he shifted, covering her body with his. His cock nudged her entrance.

"Ready?"

"You've just tasted that I'm more than ready."

Myles flexed his hips, sinking into her body, stretching and filling. At last. He took her mouth in a rough, desperate kiss as he withdrew and plunged back in, grinding his hips against her.

Piper's legs locked around him, her hips shifting to pull him even deeper. "Yes. God, yes."

"You feel so goddamned good."

"More." She nipped his lip, goading, taking his mouth in a hot, wet kiss, her tongue echoing the thrusts of his body into hers. Her hands dragged down his back, digging into his taut ass, urging him faster, harder. With every primal stroke, she tightened around him, dragging out the glorious, erotic friction of his cock moving within her, until her muscles began to quiver and pulse. The orgasm rolled through her, an unbridled storm. She cried out, body clamping around him. Above her, he stiffened, and she felt the heat of his own release as he poured into her.

Breath coming hard, Myles dropped his brow to hers. "I'm pretty sure that makes you most thoroughly mine, Mrs. Stewart."

Piper tipped her face up to kiss him. "I don't know, it might require several rounds to really take."

A chuckle rumbled through his chest. "It's best to be thorough in these matters."

"Damn straight. Although as first times go, that was…"

"The best sex of my life."

She sighed, exhausted and sated. "Glad it wasn't just me."

"Oh, I'm pretty sure that was entirely you." He rolled just far enough off her that he didn't squish her when he collapsed. "What was that you did there at the end?"

"Kegels."

"That thing you're supposed to do for bladder strength?"

Piper snorted. "They have other uses."

"I fully support those other uses. At every available opportunity." He nuzzled her shoulder.

She rolled into him, laying her left hand over his heart, looking at the rings glinting in the candlelight. Other than her pearls, they were the only thing either of them was still wearing. She liked having that visible symbol of unity.

"What's going through that busy brain of yours?" he asked.

"I was just wondering if it would've been that amazing if we hadn't been married first."

"How's that?"

"I don't know. You said yourself you felt some kind of primal satisfaction at the idea of claiming me as your wife. Did it live up to your expectations?"

His lips quirked in a rakish smile. "Honey, if you have to ask that, I did something wrong."

She laughed as he ran a hand down her leg, pulling it over his hip and proving he'd be ready to go again in very short order. But she didn't want to be distracted from this. Not yet. "No, I mean…do you feel like I'm more yours because of this," she flexed her ring hand, "than you would have without? Does this change how you feel about me? About us?"

Myles studied her, running a hand through her hair. "You mean does being married amp up what I feel for you in some artificial way, like taking on a role in a play?"

Piper didn't know whether to be pleased or terrified that he'd so easily read between the lines. "Yeah. I mean, it would be easy to get caught up in the whole thing."

"Do you think you are?" His expression held no judgment, and that made it easier to speak the truth.

"No. I know that I love you. I knew I loved you before you sang your vows to me—although if I hadn't, that would've done it. You are my perfect match, and I just…I just want to make sure I'm not in this alone."

He pressed his lips to hers. "Definitely not alone. And trust me when I say, I've never had any doubts about the veracity of what I feel for you."

Then say the words.

He didn't. But the tiny, scared part of her that needed to hear it lapsed into silence as he proceeded to show her.

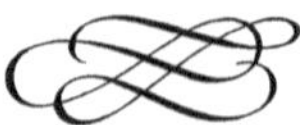

CHAPTER 11

"HOW ARE WE EVEN supposed to know where to begin?" Piper wailed.

Myles slid an arm around his wife and followed her gaze, taking in her bedroom, which looked like a tornado had ripped through. Which it sort of had, given the frenzy with which she'd packed for their honeymoon. "Okay, so it's going to be a lot. But there's no rule that says we have to get everything moved today. We don't even have to get it all this weekend." And thank God for it. Piper's house was eighteen hundred square feet of *stuff*. Pictures on every wall, furniture shoved cheek-by-jowl into every room. He had space in his place —their place—but just getting all of her things packed up was going to be a major undertaking. Maybe he could talk her into doing a little purging in the process.

Myles considered, briefly, calling up their friends to ask for help, but after all the work they'd put in on the wedding, it didn't seem quite fair to draft them for the sucktastic job of moving, too.

Her shoulders slumped. "I should've started on this before the wedding."

"In your defense, it's not like you really had time."

"I don't feel like there's time now. Two days back at work felt like two weeks. Why didn't we stay in the Caribbean?"

"Getting back into the groove at work after any legitimate time off always feels worse." The paper hadn't exactly been a mess when they'd returned, but it'd definitely proved that he couldn't just leave any of his current people at the helm and expect things to run like clockwork. "It's just going to take a little while to find the new rhythm, that's all."

Piper turned and burrowed into him. "I'm so tired. After all the stress of the wedding and the honeymoon—which was fantastic, but let's face it, not long enough and certainly not spent resting."

"Long, glorious days and nights of not resting," Myles agreed reverently, feeling his body stir at the memory.

"I'd almost kill for a weekend to do just...nothing."

"Well, there's nothing that says we have to do this now."

She lifted her head, pinning him with a Look. "Don't you balk now, buddy boy. You married me. Those vows apply in sickness and health and through moving."

Myles laughed. "I'm not trying to get out of it. I'm just saying we've got time. Pack up your clothes, your toiletries, whatever you can't live without. Get that settled. And you can take your time with packing up the rest. And once we've figured out what to keep, what to toss or sell, we can hire movers to deal with the rest."

"Movers?" she asked hopefully.

"Movers."

"You say the sweetest things." She wound her arms around his neck and kissed him, effectively derailing him from the task at hand for the next little bit.

He began to back her toward the bed conveniently at her back.

Piper stopped, breaking the kiss. "Oh no. You are not seducing me right now. We have work to do, Myles Stewart."

Unrepentant, he grinned. "It was worth a try."

"Go make yourself useful and pull the suitcases and bags out of the attic. The ladder is in the hall."

"Yes, ma'am."

By the time he came back, she'd made an

even bigger mess of the bed, having emptied the dresser drawers onto the comforter.

"Is there any particular way you want this done?" he asked.

"Cram whatever you can into whichever bag. I'm not fussy."

Myles started with a pile of scrubs, efficiently stuffing a duffel. "I can get the rest of the dresser if you want to start on the closet."

"Okay." She disappeared into its depths.

Scanning the walls, he noted the display of Playbills grouped around what he thought of as a little starlet style dressing table. There were a ton of them.

"Are these all the shows you've been in?"

"Most of them. I'm missing a few from high school. But everything I've done at The Madrigal."

"Which role was your favorite?"

"No question. Betty in *White Christmas*." She flounced out of the closet and flashed him a sassy grin. "Because it brought me you."

"Points for stroking my ego. But seriously. Is that really your favorite role?"

"I suppose not. My favorite was probably Elphaba in *Wicked*."

"Why?"

"Because she's one of the ultimate examples of love and forgiveness and being able to shake away your past and live a better life."

"It's ironic."

"What is?"

"We were both looking for that. And I consider myself so goddamned lucky to have found it."

She emerged from the closet, her eyes suspiciously glassy as she crossed over and gave him a hard kiss. "We make our own luck."

Because he couldn't bear the idea of her tears, even happy ones, he shot her a wicked grin. "Luck isn't what I feel like making just now."

"Behave, Mr. Stewart, and maybe I'll reward you later."

He heaved a theatrical sigh and sent her

back to the closet with a pat to her ass. *Back to the dresser.* "You know, I realize this is the first time I've seen your bedroom."

"Well, we didn't spend much time here. Your place was more private and there really just wasn't a lot of time."

"A part of me keeps forgetting that. On some levels, I feel like we've been together way longer. And on others, I realize there's still tons to learn about you. Like why you have a purple leopard print thong." He dangled the item in question from one finger.

Unruffled, she shrugged. "It was part of a multipack and I really liked the stripes and polka dots that came with it."

"You realize I'll want everything in this drawer modeled, right?"

"A great deal of what's in that drawer is not worth modeling."

"Not when you're the model. You make everything look amazing. Besides, the entire point of all of this is for me to take it off, and we've got an entire house to christen."

"Ambitious, are we?"

"No. Practical. If I were ambitious, I'd say we should christen all of this place, too."

She came out of the closet, one brow arched in a *Really?* sort of way that got his blood pumping. Oh, who was he kidding? Just her breathing got his blood pumping.

"I've changed my mind," he said. "I am ambitious." He started to advance on her.

She pointed an imperious hand toward the increasing mountain of clothes on the bed. "Pack."

"The clothes aren't going anywhere."

"Exactly, which is why you need to—"

He cut off her protest with his mouth, sliding his hands down her back and over that luscious ass so he could pull her closer, rocking his hips into hers. At the press of his arousal, she stopped fighting. Surrendering on a moan, her own hands skated under his shirt. She tore her mouth away so she could shove the shirt up and over his head. "We have to be fast. There's work to do."

"I can do fast."

He stripped her shirt off, reaching behind her back to release the clasp of her bra with a single flick of his fingers.

"You're awfully good at that," she murmured.

"In high school, my friends and I had a contest sometimes to see how many bras we could unhook with a flick just going down the halls."

Piper pulled back to look at him as he slid the straps down her shoulders and off. "So you just popped girls' bras randomly?"

"Yeah. I'm not real proud to admit that I held the record."

"That's—"

"Completely juvenile and stupid. I know. But it makes for fast access for this." He bent his head to take one of her nipples into his mouth.

Her hands dove into his hair. "God. I find that I can't really complain about the end result."

He smiled, and shifted to lave the other breast. And his phone went off.

She stilled, hands still gripping his hair. "Do you have to get that?"

With a disappointed sigh, he pressed a kiss to the hollow between her breasts. "Unfortunately, yes." He fished out the phone, mouthing *I'll be quick*, as he answered. "Stewart."

"Hey Myles. Sorry to bother you, but we've got a problem."

He listened to Wes outlined the issue, then asked a few questions about troubleshooting and thunked his head against the wall.

"What was that?" Wes asked.

"Nothing. I'm on my way."

When he turned around, Piper was already slipping her bra back on.

"I'm sorry."

"For leaving me unsatisfied or bailing on moving?" But her tolerant smile took the sting out.

"Both. The paper's a bitchy mistress." He blew out a breath. "I don't know how long this will take."

"It's fine. I can deal with packing my stuff

and getting the clothes and whatnot put away at the house. Go deal with your emergency."

No guilt and only a tiny bit of disappointment. God, what a woman.

"I'll get takeout for dinner so we don't have to think about it. And as soon as I get home, we'll pick up where I left off and make absolutely certain you're satisfied. As many times as necessary."

"Promises, promises," she sang.

He pressed a fast kiss to her lips. "Always."

"Mom, what are you doing here?" Piper struggled to inject some pleasure into the surprise. She'd hope to come home to someone, but that definitely hadn't been her mother. Myles had been forced to work late all week, putting out fires at the paper. Given that her mom was parked in the driveway, obviously that trend was continuing. So much for a post-work, stress relief quickie.

"Do I need a reason to come see my daughter?"

Um, yes. But Piper didn't give voice to the thought. Instead she stepped forward to give her mom a hug. "It's good to see you. Come in."

She unlocked the door and led Twyla into the kitchen. The house was a wreck, a fact Piper had been able to live with until her mother walked inside. Now all she could see was the explosion of boxes there'd been no time to unpack.

"Good Lord. You haven't gotten all this stuff put away?"

Piper fought the automatic defensiveness. "It's a work in progress. My place is still a long way from packed up. There wasn't time before the wedding, and we've only been back a little over a week."

Twyla stepped past her, eyes skimming the living room, which, while comfortable, still very much said 'bachelor'. "Have you gotten *any* of your stuff properly moved in?"

"Clothes, toiletries, some kitchen stuff. The

essentials that could easily be gotten out of the floor. I've been going to my place a little bit every day after work to keep packing things up, but it's slow going. I'm so tired. I feel like it's been go go go go go since we got engaged, and it's all starting to catch up with me. As soon as everything's packed up at my house, we're getting actual movers. But we still have to sort out what's staying, what's going and all that jazz, since there's not room here for everything from my house and everything he has."

Twyla made an elegant sniff of disapproval, but let the subject drop. "What will you be doing with your house? Selling or trying to rent it out?"

"I haven't decided yet." She wasn't quite ready to let go of her place. She didn't really know why. Myles had the bigger house, so there was no question where they'd live. And he'd given her carte blanche to do whatever she needed or wanted in order to feel more at home in their place. But she felt strange making decisions about the house without him.

They'd decided so fast that this marriage would be something real, and there'd been no bumps in that road, so that rather than feeling real, it felt...surreal. She didn't want to acknowledge the niggling sense of doubt and she sure as hell didn't want to examine it. But it was there, keeping her from fully investing in the marital reality of household meshing. So she hadn't done that much to move in, which meant she felt more like she was on an extended stayover rather than actually living here. The whole thing left her unsettled.

Not that there'd been time to talk to him about it. After all the intense one-on-one time during the honeymoon, she felt like she'd barely seen him the last week. She couldn't help wondering if their honeymoon period was already over and worrying about what that might mean. But she'd go to her grave before admitting any of that to her mother.

"Well, it's a lovely house. These counters are beautiful. What are they? Soapstone?" Twyla set her enormous purse on said counters and began to rummage.

"I believe so," Piper said carefully, struggling valiantly not to remember exactly what she and her new husband had been doing on that spot the night before. The composition of the counters had been far less a concern than the convenience of their height.

Twyla produced a small binder. "I wanted to bring you this."

"What is it?"

"It's all the cards from your reception."

"What cards?"

Exasperation flickered over her face. "We had a station, remember? Where all the guests could write their well wishes or advice for you. I organized them in an album."

Piper had missed that entirely. Then again, Myles had completely stolen the show. "That was really thoughtful, Mom. Thank you."

She flipped the book open and read the first card, written in her mother's familiar, looping script. Recipe for a happy husband: Leave discussion of your bad days and personal problems to your friends, be a cheerful, happy harbor for your spouse, and always have a hot meal ready and waiting.

"How very 1950s," Piper remarked, unable to rein in the sarcasm.

"My mother gave me that advice when I got married, and it's solid. Your father and I have been happily married for thirty-five years. You'd do well to emulate it. The last thing Myles is going to want to hear about when he gets home from a long day is whatever gross thing you had to deal with at work."

Healing being such a messy business and all. But this time she managed to keep the thought to herself.

"Home should be a pleasant, non-stressful place for him, and he'll always be happy to come back to it, no matter what he's been dealing with."

The whole thing sounded like a recipe for denial of reality to Piper, but she was past the point where she tried to get her mom to see another viewpoint. She'd just be wasting her breath. "Well, thank you for the advice. I'm sure the rest of the album will be interesting reading."

She dug back in the purse. "I also wanted to bring you this. It's a collection of all our family recipes, including all the ones from Nanna and Grandma Sylvia."

Now this Piper could show genuine pleasure over. She pounced on the box in excitement. "Does this include Nanna's recipe for Beef Concern?"

"It does."

Piper had been trying to duplicate the casserole for years, but her grandmother had held on to some secret ingredient. Getting the full recipe was a rite of passage in her family. "Thank you!" Piper hugged her.

Her mother's pleased expression shifted to mild exasperation as she pulled back and looked into Piper's face. "Heavens. Did you put on *any* makeup this morning?"

And we're back to the norm. "That was quite a few hours ago, Mom."

Twyla stepped back and picked up her purse. "You ought to freshen up before Myles gets home. And maybe put on something other than your scrubs. You smell like antiseptic."

Piper sighed. She didn't have the energy for this fight today. "Yes, ma'am."

Once her mother was safely out the door, Piper opened the recipe box and began flipping through, looking for the one she wanted. Plucking it out, she skimmed over the ingredient list. Miracle of miracles, they actually had everything on hand, so she set about pulling the casserole together for supper. Not because she thought Myles was Ward Cleaver but because she'd had a crap day and *she* wanted comfort food. Once it was safely in the oven, she did go shower and change—for herself, not because she thought Myles cared—then summoned some determination to empty a few more boxes.

"Piper?"

"Back here!" she called. She'd just finished up putting the last of her paperbacks onto the bookcase they'd moved into the guest room when he stuck his head through the door.

"Something smells amazing, other than you." He tugged her up off the floor and into a warm kiss that untangled some of the knots of stress from the day.

"It's Beef Concern."

Myles made a comical face. "Should I *be* concerned?"

"It's just called Beef Concern. I don't know why. It's my grandmother's recipe. I guess because it's the casserole she makes whenever she's concerned about somebody."

"Are you concerned about somebody?"

She started to mention the seemingly endless string of non-compliant patients, who'd decided to take attitude and blame their lack of responsibility on her, which had left her waspish and hangry. But then she stopped herself. "I just wanted some comfort food and I figured you'd appreciate a meal that wasn't take out after all the hours you'd been putting in."

He beamed at her. "You are the sweetest thing. I've been looking forward to coming home to this smile all day." He kissed her again, but Piper's mind was circling back to her mother's questionable advice.

"How long until dinner?" Myles wanted to know.

"Maybe another twenty minutes. I was going to unpack a few more boxes."

"Well you could do that," he conceded. "Or we could put that time to other use."

As it was exactly what she'd wanted when she got home, Piper wasn't about to say no to that. "That, Mr. Stewart, is an excellent idea."

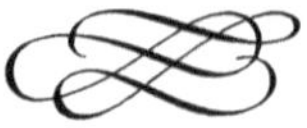

"OMAR SENT PO-BOYS."

Myles pulled his brain out of the inDesign template as Simone set a bag of takeout on the edge of his desk. The scent of grease and spice wafting from the containers had his mouth watering and his stomach rumbling. A clear reminder that he hadn't had more than a pack of crackers from his drawer for lunch.

"I figured you weren't leaving any time soon, so I'd better put food in front of you before you keeled over."

He took off his reading glasses and tossed them next to his keyboard. Stubble rasped against his palms as he rubbed both hands over his face. "What time is it?"

"Nearly six."

He hadn't even noticed when the rest of his staff left the office. "I need to call Piper and tell her not to wait dinner on me."

"Her car was still at the clinic when I drove by."

Well, that was something. At least she wasn't waiting on him. Had he been home anywhere approaching a reasonable hour at any point in the last two weeks? Barely. He'd been so damned busy with the paper, there'd hardly been opportunity to do more than sleep in the same bed. Something had to give, and he sure as hell didn't want it to be his nascent marriage.

"Just as well you came back. I wanted to talk to you about something."

Simone braced herself. "It something going wrong with your access to the trust?"

"What? No. Everything's fine there. I should

be granted access in a few days." Thank God. He needed that burden off his shoulders. "No, I wanted to talk about some of the issues that came up running things while I was gone. You'll need to make some changes in how you handle things if you're to take on more responsibility around here."

"Myles, with respect, you're a good friend, and I love you. But I don't want more responsibility around here."

"What?" Oh, dear Lord. Was she quitting?

"If your honeymoon taught me anything, it's that I'm a reporter, not an editor. I never had that desire to mold and create a publication like you did. At least not the same way. I took this job in part because I wanted to get a chance to explore a different kind of journalism than I got in the city. But I also took it because it would be less demanding in a lot of ways and would give me the chance to actually have a life."

Ironic, since his position here meant he had less of one.

Because he needed something to do with his

hands, Myles unwrapped one of the po-boys and bit in. Fried shrimp. The breading was light and crunchy, the spice and salt a glorious counterpoint to the crisp lettuce and creamy mayo. God bless Omar. "And would that life be including seeing Omar Buckley on a more personal basis?"

"It would. As you well know, since you're not blind. But he's only part of it. I'm writing."

"Well, yes, of course you're writing. You handed in two stories this morning. The markups are in your email."

"No, I mean really writing. Fiction." Her eyes shone with excitement.

Despite the fatigue, Myles felt his interest pique. "Yeah? What genre?"

"Romantic suspense at the moment. Though I've got several other things kicking around in my brain."

"I didn't know you had aspirations in that direction."

Simone laughed, her rich voice like a bubble of caramel. "Neither did I. But I love it. Really love it, the way you love running this paper. And I don't want to take on anything that's going to interfere with pursuing that. I certainly don't mind helping out, when necessary. I know a paper like this means a lot of cross-training and interchangeability, but this isn't about having a sub so you can go on a proper honeymoon. You're really wanting someone to take over a lot of the responsibility for the paper on a more permanent basis."

"You're not wrong. I want an assistant editor."

"It won't be me."

He leaned back in his chair. "Well, shit."

"Is that a deal breaker for my position here?"

"Of course not. If it were, I'd have brought all of it up when I hired you in the first place. But I've got to figure something out. I can't keep working like this."

"Won't things settle down once you pay off your investor?"

"I'm afraid we're a long way from settling down, period. For good reasons. The paper's having a growth spurt, and that's great. But I need more help to manage it. I could outsource some of it, but that would defeat the purpose of what I'm doing here. I want to keep my business here in the community, as much as possible. To do that, I need a proper assistant editor. You were the closest to qualified of all the staff to do what I want, and if you don't want it, I have to find someone else."

"Is there anybody locally who might suit?"

"No one with the necessary experience, even if there might be interest. And I'm inclined to be choosy in who I bring in from the outside. Not everyone would appreciate a community like Wishful."

Simone considered as she worked her way through her own po-boy. "You need a Clark Kent."

"How's that?"

"A reporter with small town roots, who went off to the big city like we did and is ready for a change."

The wheels in Myles' head began to turn. "No...not a Clark Kent. A Vanessa Clark."

"Who?"

"Vanessa Clark. She's a reporter I worked with at *The Times* in Seattle. Originally from a little town in Nebraska. A real hot shot. Bright, capable, with a definite eye for climbing the ladder. She left about the same time I did for Philly. I wonder where she landed..."

"What makes you think she'd be a good fit?"

"Because she was just as disgusted with the corporate politics as I was, and she was interested in moving to a smaller paper."

Shoving his food away, Myles grabbed his keyboard and pulled up Facebook. It took a few minutes to sort through the results, but he finally tracked down his former colleague—now Vanessa Clark-Ellis—in Baltimore.

"Let's see. Got married three years ago. And...apparently, had a baby a few months ago. Working at the *Baltimore Sun* now. Definitely not the smaller paper she talked about."

"What's she working on?"

He clicked over to the *Sun's* website and searched out her work. "Some political stuff most recently, with a gap when she was probably on maternity leave. Looks like the crime beat before that."

"Not exactly the kind of thing you want to mess with if you've got a little one," Simone observed.

"It's probably a long shot since she's married, but worth a phone call, at least."

"What's the husband do?"

"Wife." He shifted the monitor to point out the Facebook cover photo showing two smiling brides, then clicked a few more links. "Looks like she's some kind of artist. Metalwork. Sculpture. That kind of thing."

"The Chadwick is always looking for new exhibits..."

Myles grinned at her, liking that she was thinking along the same lines as he was. "So they are."

Simone balled up her wrapper and made a three pointer into the trash. "Well, good luck. I leave you to your sleuthing now that I'm confident you aren't going to pass out of starvation at your desk."

"Thanks for dinner, Sim."

"See you tomorrow."

He was already eyeballs deep in a plan by the time she walked out the door.

"Dear God, it's worse than last year," Shelby groaned. "When will someone manage to find a way to vaccinate for the stomach flu?"

"Sadly, it doesn't work that way," Miranda said.

"Please tell me we're done with everything," Piper begged. "I don't want to think about how many bodily fluids I cleaned up today. I just want to go home, have a bath, and face plant straight into bed. Maybe with a brief detour for food, if Myles put on dinner." Not that he'd been home early enough for that at any point, but surely the Universe would see fit to grant her a miracle after such a shitty day. It was only fair.

"I'm pretty sure we've disinfected every centimeter of the building," Keisha replied.

"Good call on the hydrogen peroxide wipes and spray," Miranda added. "Maybe it'll help keep us from getting it."

"Hope springs eternal," Piper muttered. "See y'all tomorrow."

She drove home on autopilot, head feeling swimmy from exhaustion. Myles' car wasn't in the garage. Of course. Why should she have expected otherwise? That likely meant there wouldn't be dinner. Given the fresh roiling in her stomach, she needed to put something in it.

The fridge was embarrassingly bare. Two lonely eggs, some spinach past its prime, a half package of lunch meat that smelled off, and coffee creamer. The pantry wasn't much better for ready-made fare. Cereal was about the only option. There wasn't even canned soup.

Sighing, she called Myles.

"Stewart." It was his editor-in-chief voice,

which meant he was deep in work mode.

"Hey, it's me."

There was a pause, during which Piper heard the clatter of a keyboard. "Hey you. What time is—oh crap. I meant to call you an hour ago to say I'd be late."

"I just got home myself. It was a terrible, horrible, no good, very bad day." She could hear the whine in her own voice and couldn't muster enough give-a-damn to stop it.

"What happened?"

"Stomach flu epidemic. You don't want to hear the gory details. Just be sure to wash your hands after touching anything in public."

"Yes, ma'am." He lapsed into a silence that she'd learned meant his brain was already half back on his work. Given how much he loved his job and how hard he worked, Piper was working on not being offended by that. But just now it was kinda hard.

"I didn't actually call to gripe about my day. I wanted to beg you to pick up take out on your way home."

"Oh. Maybe you should call for Chinese. I'm not sure you want to wait on me."

"You're going to be a while, then?"

"Working on something that could be huge for the paper."

She held in a sigh, missing the guy who'd juggled everything in his schedule to spend every spare moment with her before they got married. "Okay. I'm pretty wiped. I may be asleep by the time you get home."

"Yeah, don't wait up on my account. You sound half dead on your feet. If I don't make it home before you crash, I'll see you in the morning, okay?"

Piper swallowed down her disappointment. She'd wanted some comfort and support tonight. It had been a blanket fort and foot rub worthy kind of day. She waited to speak until she could keep her tone even. "Be careful on your way home."

"I will. Promise. Night, Piper."

The dial tone interrupted her goodnight.

Great. No food. No husband. A lousy end to

a craptastic day.

As she ran a hot bath, she didn't have the energy for her usual optimism. This sucked big donkey balls. Since they'd come home from their honeymoon, he'd worked longer and longer hours, becoming more and more consumed at the paper. Other than the fact that they managed to share a bed for a few hours a night, the last week hadn't felt much different than those three months of hiatus.

Was this what his normal life was? Piper realized she had no idea. During their months of working on the show, they hadn't talked much about his business. She really had no idea what he'd had to do in order to make time for the show. As well as she understood him on some fronts, there was a great deal she didn't know about the man she'd married.

Was this what would've happened to their relationship if it had gone the normal course of dating instead of them diving headlong into marriage? Her being gradually pushed to the side in the name of his work? Zing or no zing, she wouldn't have put up with this from a boyfriend for very long. She wasn't some needy, codependent wuss, but she expected to do more than share the same address and semi-regular orgasms with her husband.

Stripping out of her scrubs, Piper slid into the water, hissing as the heat burned her toes.

Surely things would settle down once access to the trust went through and his investor was paid off. This pace he was setting for himself wasn't sustainable for any kind of life.

As the heat soaked into her aching muscles, a horrible thought popped into her brain.

What if he was deliberately taking on all these long hours because he'd realized he didn't actually want to be married to her? Had the bloom worn off so soon? Had he been disappointed to find out that she wasn't crazy, fun-loving, optimistic Piper all the time? Surely he'd realized before he walked down the aisle that there was more to her. Hadn't he?

But then how would he have known? When had he ever seen any other side of her? They hadn't spent enough time together for him to know what she was like under other circumstances. He might understand the heart of her, but what if the everyday reality was a disappointment? Had they failed in their marriage before their first month was even up?

Feeling suddenly overheated and queasy, Piper boosted herself out of the bath.

I'm exhausted and not in the right frame of mind. I'll just go on to bed, get a good night's sleep, and when I'm calmer and more rational, we'll talk about it like sane adults.

But having a plan of action did nothing to quell the rising nausea. She bolted for the toilet, barely making it before her stomach revolted. Little remained of her lunch, but she continued to heave, stomach cramping and twisting, wringing out every last drop of bile and acid, until, at last, she lay panting on the floor, cheek pressed to the cold tile.

Looked like her luck, along with their honeymoon period, had finally run out.

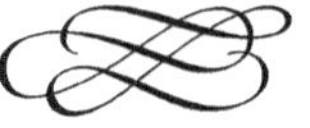

CHAPTER 13

MYLES FELT HIS BLOOD sing. He hadn't had cause to pull out his investigative reporter skills since he moved back to Mississippi—uncovering Piper's matchmaking scheme during the play notwithstanding. He'd just sussed out everything he could possibly need to know about Vanessa Clark's current circumstances. The combination of her new daughter and noted discontent with her role at *The Baltimore Sun,* along with those small-town roots, meant he had a shot at wooing her to Wishful. He'd used the same methods on Simone, though that process had been easier because they'd still kept in touch.

As he drove home late that night, he knew his mind would be far too wired to sleep. He'd look in on Piper and hole up in his home office, start working out the specifics to his plan. This wasn't about money. No way in hell could he offer her the kind of salary she'd be accustomed to at a metropolitan paper with serious resources. So he had to play other cards. The benefits of small town life. The chance to take a bigger role and more control in the publication. The opportunity to raise her child in a town where the most serious crime in the last six months had been grand theft auto by a couple of high schoolers looking to joyride. Even connections to the Southern art scene for her wife. He'd get on the latter tomorrow and see if Peter Chadwick would reach out to Leslie Clark-Ellis about the possibility of a show. Might as well get Wishful in both their minds before he made the call.

Piper had left the lights on for him.

Thoughtful. Because the po-boy Simone brought had been hours ago, Myles tugged open the fridge in search of leftover Chinese. Nothing.

Huh. She must've changed her mind. Damn, we need to go to the grocery.

He scribbled out a list while he was thinking about it, then walked quietly down the hall, not wanting to wake her.

The light from the bedroom shone into the hall. Myles glanced at his watch. Nearly midnight. Surely, she hadn't waited up for him.

But Piper wasn't curled up in bed reading or watching TV. The door to the bathroom was ajar, the light on in there. He pushed it open the rest of the way, expecting to see her getting ready for bed—and felt his heart stop at the sight of a long, naked leg stretched along the floor.

"Piper!" He bolted into the room.

She lay naked on the bath mat in front of the toilet, partially draped in a towel. Oh God, had she fallen? Somehow struck her head?

Myles crouched beside her, pitifully relieved to feel the warmth of living flesh when he laid a hand on her thigh. No blood. No bruising. At least half the scenarios that'd popped into his overactive mind, faded. "Piper, baby."

She slitted her eyes open, but didn't lift her head. "You're home." Her voice came out in a rusty croak.

"What the hell happened?"

Her eyes drifted shut again, as if even holding them open was too much effort. "Stomach flu. Don't touch me. You'll catch it."

"Screw that. What kind of husband would I be if I fell down on the 'in sickness' part?" Self-recriminations ricocheted through his mind for what kind of husband he'd been these past couple of weeks that he hadn't even realized she'd been getting sick.

He started to scoop her up, but she groaned in protest.

"I don't think I'm done throwing up." As if to illustrate the point, she jackknifed up, gripping the bowl and retching. Nothing came up but bile.

"Oh, honey."

Myles brought her a cold, wet washcloth and wiped her face. She groaned, a blend of pain and relief. He filled a glass from the bathroom counter and brought it back to where she lay draped on the rim, her head lolling on her arm. Sliding an arm behind her back, he lifted her to a sitting position and held the glass to her lips. "C'mon. Sip and swish."

Once her mouth was washed out, he eased her back down. "You're freezing."

"Naked. Tile floor."

"Yeah, why is that?"

"Barely made it out of the tub."

Not sure where she'd put her pajamas, he pulled one of his own shirts out of the closet. "Let's fix that." Kneeling beside her, he slipped it over her head.

"Thanks."

"Let's get you out of the floor."

"I don't think I should be far from the toilet."

"Okay then." He bent and lifted her, shifting around and settling back on the floor in the tiny room with her in his lap.

"You really shouldn't—"

"Shouldn't what? Take care of you? Sickness and health. I'm already exposed. Deal with it."

"You don't have time for this," she protested, shoving weakly at his shoulder. "You don't have time for me."

The resentment in her voice was faint but there. It rankled and fed the guilt already nipping at his heels. Did she have *any* idea what he'd had to do to spend all that time with her before the wedding? None of that was free, and he was having to pay the price for it now. Unfortunately, that meant he'd been a less than perfect spouse lately. What more did she expect him to do?

She wilted into him, pressing her clammy brow into the hollow of his throat. "That's not fair. I'm sorry. I feel awful and it makes me bitchy."

She's sick as a dog and vulnerable. Everybody says stuff they don't mean when they feel lousy.

It was on the tip of his tongue to say that this was temporary. If he could woo Vanessa into joining the staff, he'd be able to cut back and spend more time on that life Piper made him want. But the deal wasn't done yet, and Myles wasn't in the habit of making promises he didn't know he could keep. Words meant nothing unless backed up with action. He knew that better than most. So instead of dubious promises, he tightened his arms. "I know, baby. I'm sorry. I'm sorry about so many things right now."

Piper stirred, making a noise of question.

He held her in place. "Doesn't matter. I'm here. I'll rearrange things so I can stay home with you while you're dealing with all this. You shouldn't be alone when you're this sick." God knew what he'd have to give up to pull it off, but she was worth it.

"SHOULD YOU ACTUALLY BE HERE?" Miranda gave Piper a critical once over.

"I look worse than I feel." It was the truth. Mostly. She'd been able to keep some oatmeal down, and as she'd made it out the door before Myles started the coffee, nothing else had set her precarious stomach off.

"You look about two steps up from warmed-over death," Shelby observed.

Piper made a face. "Thanks. You looked awesome, too, after you had the flu last year."

"Just don't give it to any of us," Miranda said.

"Myles has been home taking care of me for days and didn't catch it. You should be fine." Which had been both wonderful and irritating. She was a crap patient, and she knew it. For all that she was great taking care of others, she didn't tolerate it well herself, and Myles seemed to be on some kind of crusade to prove something by playing mother hen. Still, it had been great to spend some actual time with him, even if it had taken dire illness to drag him away from his beloved paper.

And now she was glad to get back to work. Resolute, Piper picked up the first patient chart of the day and went to call Mr. Clemmons back. The moment she opened the waiting room door, the scent of cigar smoke assailed her, making her stomach lurch.

No. Absolutely not. I am not throwing up again.

Eyes scanning the room for the asshole ignoring the non-smoking rule, she swallowed back the nausea. No one was smoking. And other than Mr. Clemmons, the only other people in the waiting room were a mom with two sniffling children and an elderly woman. None of them were likely cigar smokers.

What the hell?

When she was certain she could speak without anything but words coming out, Piper fixed a friendly smile on her face. "Mr. Clemmons, come on back and let me get your vitals."

She took him into triage, grateful to be back to routine. Temperature. Blood pressure.

Oxygen levels. Nature of complaint. That done, she placed him in room one and wandered back out to the office area.

"Does anybody else smell smoke?"

"I swear to God, the burnt popcorn smell is gone," Shelby protested. "It's been days."

"No, not that. I smell cigar smoke. But Mr. Clemmons doesn't smoke, and I kind of doubt any of the others in the waiting room are lighting up stogies."

"Stranger things have happened."

"Randolph Driscoll was in yesterday," Miranda said. "You know he chain smokes cigars."

"Maybe somebody should check the plants in the waiting room to see if he happened to use one for an ash tray."

"I don't smell anything," said Shelby.

Piper stepped up behind her at the counter that opened out front. The smell all but knocked her back two steps. "Seriously? You don't smell that?" Her gorge rose, and she covered her mouth, stepping back.

"Oh, no. I know that face." Shelby rolled

back in her chair and picked up the disinfectant spray, brandishing it like a weapon. "Back away."

"Piper, join me in three for a minute." Miranda waited until she followed all the way to the room in the back.

When she shut the door behind them, Piper began to worry. "Am I in trouble?"

"Not with me. Sit down. You're looking peaked."

"I'm fine. I just want to get back to work."

"Piper." Miranda didn't often pull out the trauma surgeon voice, but when she did, everyone was inclined to listen.

Piper sat, crossing her arms in defense of...she had no idea what. "I'm telling you, I'm not contagious."

"No, you're not."

"Great. We're agreed. Why are we back here?"

"I don't think you've had the stomach flu."

"Excuse me, I've been puking my guts up for five days."

"Gastroenteritis doesn't tend to last that long. The strain that's been running rampant around here lasts forty-eight hours. And it's highly contagious. There's no way Myles wouldn't have caught it if that's what you had."

"So I had some other strain. What does it matter?"

Miranda continued, hazel eyes level on Piper's. "A stomach virus isn't going to result in your being able to smell evidence of a patient who was here nearly twenty-four hours ago. One who definitely wasn't smoking in the waiting room."

Feeling mulish, Piper scowled. "I'm telling you, there's something out there. The rest of you have stuffed up sinuses."

"You're overlooking the obvious diagnosis here." Miranda watched her, a faintly amused expression on her face that made Piper feel like the class idiot.

"I have no idea what you're talking about."

"Honey, when was your last period?"

Piper blinked, taken aback by the question.

"I don't know. I'd have to look at a calendar. But I'm not pregnant, Miranda. I'm on birth control."

"So say members of the one percent all the time."

"I can't possibly be pregnant. I've only been married for three weeks."

And I should have started right when we got back from our honeymoon.

The blood drained out of her head. "I can't be pregnant," she whispered.

"We can find out for sure and put your mind at ease."

"Not here. If I do it here, everyone will know. If I am, I can't risk it getting back to Myles before I have a chance to talk to him."

And say what exactly? Hey, I know we went into this with an exit strategy in mind, and we talked about it being real, but guess what? Things just got complicated.

"Not something you two have discussed?"

"I don't even know if he wants kids." She

thought of him with Preston. Surely, he wanted them. Someday, at least.

"Be right back." Miranda disappeared, coming back a minute later with two boxes in her hand. Pregnancy tests. "Take these. Go home. If anybody asks, you're still not quite up to being back at work. Find out for certain before you start flipping out."

Numb, she slid them into her pocket. "Thanks."

"I'm here if you need me."

Somehow, Piper made it out the door and all the way home without giving in to the panic. Myles had taken her advice and gone on to the office. For once, she was grateful he wasn't home. No reason he should be witness to the imminent freak out that would turn out to be over nothing. Because there was no way she could be pregnant.

But half an hour later, two identical positives proved her wrong.

Oh God. *Oh God.* How had this happened? She'd taken the damned pills like clockwork.

She'd counted on them working as intended. And now she was pregnant with the child of a man who, despite all his actions to the contrary, had never even said he loved her. A man who might very well be already regretting his decision to go along with her crazy plan, for all that he'd been sweet and attentive taking care of her the last week.

He hadn't signed on for this. Neither had she. This was supposed to be a friendship with marital benefits and the real potential for more. A fun adventure with an escape hatch should either of them change their mind. It wasn't meant to be an instafamily.

She had to talk to him.

Her hand reached for the phone before she pulled it back. No. Not the kind of conversation to be had on the phone. He'd know the moment he heard her voice that something was wrong, and she wasn't sure she could keep it from all spilling out, fueled by the rising panic beating in her chest.

She'd go to his office. Not ideal, but there

was no way she could wait until he got home at whatever ungodly hour was necessary for him to make up the work he'd missed taking care of her. She'd go insane.

By the time she made it to *The Observer,* she'd managed to find some measure of control. It wouldn't last long, but it ought to be enough to get past his staff and into his office for a private conversation. Putting on her best *everything's fine* face, she went inside.

Patty was on the phone, but she smiled and waved Piper back toward Myles' office. With a vague sense of unreality, she walked down the hall. The blinds were drawn, but his door was open and voices spilled out.

"I love this paper. I really do. I've endured a lot of shit to get it turned around, and that's finally paying off." Myles.

Piper smiled at the satisfaction in his voice, proud that he was finally getting what he wanted. But there was something else in his tone she couldn't quite put her finger on, and it had her hesitating in the hall.

"But I think I'm about to the point where I have to suck it up and admit defeat."

Defeat? What's he talking about?

"Are you sure you want to do that?" Simone asked. "I mean, you put a lot into this. Who else would've gone so far in the name of the paper?"

Simone knew about their arrangement. Knew their marriage was a means to an end to buy out Myles' investor.

Heart pounding, Piper strained to hear his response.

"Yeah, I did. And I tried really hard to believe in the possibilities. But I think it's time to cut her loose and move on. She's not who I thought she was, and I just don't have anything left to give. I can't let it be an emotional decision. It's just business."

And she remembered what he'd said when he'd come home to find her sick. *I'm sorry about so many things right now.*

Apparently, she was at the top of the list.

Piper felt her world shatter. Pain lanced through her chest, screaming down every nerve, stealing her breath. He didn't love her. The marriage she'd wanted so desperately to be real was nothing but a means to an end, and he wanted out of the deal, just as his investor had wanted out of the paper because there wasn't enough return on his investment.

It was just business.

CHAPTER 14

"I THINK I'M ABOUT to the point where I have to suck it up and admit defeat." The admission left Myles feeling exhausted. Particularly in the wake of having been home with Piper most of the last week. He didn't want to go back to the sixteen hour days and never see his wife.

"Are you sure you want to do that?" Simone asked. "I mean, you put a lot into this. Who else would've gone so far in the name of the paper?"

Setting up the potential for a show for Leslie

Clark-Ellis. Pulling together information on the local real estate market and showing how much home they could have here versus the city. Even getting information on the local schools—some of the best in the state. It had been a lot of work. But what choice did he have? Vanessa's counter offer was ludicrous. There was no way he could meet it.

"Yeah, I did. And I tried really hard to believe in the possibilities. But I think it's time to cut her loose and move on. She's not who I thought she was, and I just don't have anything left to give. I can't let it be an emotional decision. It's just business."

"So what will you do?"

"Go through the process of formal search and see who comes out of the woodwork. There's someone else out there right for the job. It'll just take more time." Meanwhile, there had to be something he could do, something he could change to make sure his marriage was still a priority.

His hand twitched toward his phone, wanting to text Piper and check on her.

Simone read his mind. "How's Piper?"

"She went back to work this morning. Grumpy as hell after being an invalid for five days. But she still looked a little green, so not sure if it'll take or not." Never in his life had he seen anyone so sick, and that included seeing some of his college roommates after a bender. She'd barely managed to keep down more than a little chicken soup, crackers, and ginger ale until day before yesterday. "I want to get things wrapped up here as much as possible, in case I need to work from home again."

"Jay had some ideas for how we could improve our work flow to allow you more freedom to work from your home office under normal circumstances."

"Yeah?" *All hail my favorite tech guy*, he thought. "I'll give him a call a little later."

Maybe there was some software or equipment he could buy in the name of work-life balance. Now that he had full access to the trust, he had some more flexibility in his spending. Though Mr. Moncreiff, the attorney who handled Gram's affairs—and Granddaddy's before that for decades—might just have a coronary if he asked to pull out any more than he already had to pay off his investor. Myles could just imagine all the thoughts about recklessness and irresponsibility floating through the old man's head.

Simone rose. "I'm off to finish the article on the new small business incentive program."

Myles blew out a breath. "I guess I'm about to shoot down Vanessa's counter offer. Might as well get it over with."

"Good luck with that."

Once she'd gone, Myles picked up his phone, thumb hovering over the keyboard. Piper had only been at work for an hour. And she'd been aggravated with his mother hen routine before she left. Maybe he'd give it a while longer before he checked in.

Shifting gears, he called Vanessa.

She answered on the second ring, her voice brisk and efficient. "Well, I didn't expect to hear from you quite so soon. I assumed you received my counter?"

"Oh, I received it. Had a good laugh." He could all but hear her bristle over the phone.

"I was perfectly serious, Myles."

"I'm sure you are. But you're coming at me with big city tactics. This is a small-town paper, V. We're doing okay, and we're growing, but we don't have the kind of resources to give you what you want."

"So what's your counter?"

"I don't have one. This is a job opportunity, not a flea market. The bottom line is that I can't give you the kind of salary you expect. I can't even offer you what you probably deserve."

"Then why exactly are we having this conversation?"

Why indeed?

"Because I think you can share my vision.

Because I think that after years of working in big city papers, you're sick of the corporate policies and having little to no say in your assignments or the overall finished product. I think you're tired of being one voice among many. I think you're questioning whether you want to raise your daughter in a place where she'll likely end up in private school. Where she's never going to have friends down the street or be able to play in the yard without direct supervision. Which is assuming you ever found an affordable place with a yard. I think you worry about her growing up so close to the cesspool of DC, and you're starting to get nostalgic about your small-town upbringing."

"You've been thinking an awful lot." Her tone was the verbal equivalent of eyes narrowed in offense.

"The fact is, Vanessa, what I'm offering here isn't just a job. It's a chance at a different way of life. You've got the package I put together on the schools, the real estate, even the art scene for your wife. It's almost the lowest cost of living in the nation, in a town that's in the middle of a renaissance. And it's a chance to get in almost at the ground floor, a chance to really influence that renaissance, that community, through this paper. An opportunity to forge ties and create something that has a more lasting and meaningful impact than an op ed piece no one will remember next week or next month. Real human journalism."

Myles took a breath. "I can do what I'm doing on my own. I've done damned well with my limited staff so far. But I want someone to share that with me V. And I wanted that to be you." He still did, if he was honest. And that drove him to one last hail Mary pass. "Now I know you like to play hardball. You're damned good at it. I wasn't prepared to offer you any-thing more than what you've already seen, but on the off-chance that this makes a difference, I'm willing to throw in ten percent ownership of the paper."

"Why would you do that? *The Observer* is your baby. You love that paper."

"I do. I've put my blood, sweat, tears, and money into it. I've *just* paid off my original investor so that I have sole ownership." Okay, not a hundred percent true until tomorrow, but there was no reason to quibble. "But I love my wife more." The admission echoed through him like a gong. He loved Piper. He'd known it for weeks, but it was the first time he'd said it aloud. And it felt good to say it, to admit it to someone. Myles hated that it hadn't first been to Piper herself. Something he'd rectify as soon as he saw her again.

"I didn't know you were married."

"For less than a month. But she's the best thing in my life, and it's not worth working myself into the ground and losing her. I need help. And if that's not going to be you, I need to find someone else."

That was it. Everything he had rolled into probably the most honest pitch he could make. Myles held his breath waiting to see if she'd bite.

Vanessa was quiet for a long moment. "When do I start?"

"THANK YOU FOR SEEING ME." Piper clasped her hands, hoping Gram Stewart wouldn't try to take one and find out exactly how sweaty they were.

Suzanne stepped back from the front door Piper had been surprised she answered herself. In a place like this, she'd expected a butler or something.

"I have to admit I was surprised to hear from you. After all the hoopla of the wedding, I expected you and Myles to go to ground for a while and hide."

So did I. Piper bit back the pain of what might have been. Now wasn't the time to think about how different reality was from what she'd expected for their marriage.

She stepped inside, her heels echoing in the

high-ceilinged foyer. "You and I have some business to discuss."

"Oh? Well, you'd best come on back to the parlor."

Parlor. Because Suzanne Stewart's house—mansion, really—was big enough to have a formal parlor.

I am not in Kansas anymore, Toto.

Suzanne gestured for her to take a seat.

Piper moved to a tufted settee and sat, smoothing her skirt. She'd dressed carefully for this meeting, as much to make a good impression as to armor up against a formidable opponent. For all she'd praised Piper's moxie and gone to the trouble of putting on the wedding, Piper was under no illusions that Suzanne was anything less than the staunch matriarch of the Stewart clan. The last thing she wanted was to come across as upset and terrified as she actually was.

"Shall I ring for coffee?"

Piper's traitorous stomach gave a lurch at the thought. Only her years of acting experience prevented her from outright wincing. "No, thank you." She didn't expect to be staying long enough for beverages anyway.

Suzanne folded her hands. "Well then, out with it. You've clearly got something on your mind."

Piper reached into her purse and pulled out the manila envelope that had ridden like an executioner in her passenger seat all the way from Wishful. At her request, Tucker had—reluctantly—drawn the contents up in a hurry. He couldn't understand how necessary this step was in order for her to move forward.

She handed it over to Suzanne. "I came to bring you this."

The older woman frowned, but she didn't waste time asking obvious questions about what was in her hands, instead reaching over to a side table for a pair of reading glasses.

Piper was grateful for the brief reprieve from explaining herself. She hadn't quite figured out what to say that would be the least revealing about her current situation and the least damning to Myles. This was about setting the record straight, not hurting him.

Suzanne said nothing, reading through the short document twice before lowering it and fixing sharp blue eyes on Piper. "A post-nuptial agreement. Why?"

Summoning as much high-class hauteur as possible, Piper squared her shoulders. "Given the accusations directed at me on your discovery of our engagement, I didn't want there to be any question that I truly have no designs on Myles' money or the family fortunes."

Dismay flickered over the older woman's face. "There is no apology I can make that will suffice to repair the damage from that ill-conceived action. But I am sorry."

Piper shook her head. That hardly mattered now. She swallowed, her mouth suddenly dry as she faced telling as much of the truth as she dared. "The fact is, you were right to be suspicious. Just not for the reasons you thought."

One patrician brow winged up. And she waited.

"Our marriage *was* about money. But not for me. For Myles."

Something chilled in her expression. "How so?"

"Myles needed a large sum of cash to pay off his primary investor in the paper or he risked losing control entirely. He could have found other investors, but there was an exceptionally short timeline, so his only real option was the trust. Which, as you know, he couldn't access until he married."

Suzanne sucked in a breath. "My grandson used you?" The fury in her voice was quiet but deadly.

"I was a willing accomplice. When he told me about his problems with the paper, I'm the one who came up with the whole plan to help him save it. I was the obvious choice. We had a history because of the theater and no one would have any reason to doubt the veracity of our relationship."

"You were acting?"

That made Piper stumble. Here she couldn't

lie. "I wasn't, no. Without all of this, we'd have been dating like normal people. We're friends. Good friends. We tried being more." Because her voice wanted to shake, she paused, curling her hands to fists in her lap. "The fact is, Myles got what he needed, what he wanted, out of the arrangement. It was just business. The paper is safe, or will be after he meets with his investor tomorrow. And now I'm letting him go because I'm not what he needs or wants in the long term." She nodded toward the post-nup agreement. "I had that drawn up to make certain that there's never been any question of my wanting anything from him for having held up my end of the bargain."

Suzanne sat back. "I hardly know what to say."

"You needn't say anything. I just wanted to be sure everything was clear before things move forward."

The glasses got tossed, skittering across the table and onto the floor. "Goddamn that boy for a fool."

Piper's eyes widened, at the unexpected invective. "Please don't be angry with him. He was stuck between a rock and a hard place, and he never would have come up with this idea on his own. Credit for that goes entirely to me. Your family values business acumen. So just...focus on the fact that what he's pulled off with *The Observer* is nothing short of miraculous, and leave it at that."

"Your mind's made up?"

"My end of the deal is fulfilled. It's time for me to go."

They lapsed into a strained silence.

An ache built in Piper's throat now that she'd said her piece. If she didn't get out of here now, she was going to burst into tears, and Suzanne was the last person she wanted to see that kind of weakness. She picked up her purse and rose. "I'll see myself out."

She'd made it to the door of the parlor before Suzanne called her name.

Piper turned back, a question on her face.

When Suzanne spoke, her voice was gentler

than Piper would have expected. "You don't expect anything at all from him?"

She swallowed. "Nothing he's willing to give. The whole thing was a business arrangement. I was the only one foolish enough to bring hearts into the equation."

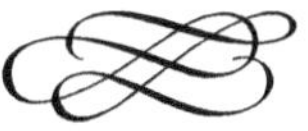

CHAPTER 15

"OKAY, I'M HEADED OUT, unless you need anything else."

Myles looked up at Patty and smiled. "No, I'm good. Thanks for all your help."

"It's what I do. And tell Piper I hope she feels better. She still looked pretty ill when she was in this morning."

Myles frowned. "This morning?"

"Yeah she stopped by around nine. Didn't you see her?"

"No."

"You've been in and out of meetings and on the phone all day. Maybe she decided not to bother you."

"Maybe," he murmured. But why would she go to the trouble of coming in if she wasn't planning on staying?

"See you tomorrow."

Preoccupied, he waved to Patty and started loading his messenger bag with the things he needed to take home for the night. Piper hadn't been at home when he popped in for lunch, so she hadn't had a relapse. Maybe Patty was right and she'd just stopped in on her way to get coffee or something at The Grind. If it had been anything important, she'd have waited for him to get done with...whatever he'd been doing when she was here.

In the mood to celebrate, Myles picked up a bottle of champagne on the way home. Between his usual editorial duties and a handful of meetings, he'd spent a fair chunk of the day getting all the details hammered out regarding hiring Vanessa. Her start date was still a little fuzzy, as she needed to sort the issue of moving with her wife, but there was an end in sight to his obsessive overworking.

And he was going home to his own wife to tell her what he should've said the day they married.

Piper, I love you.

Given her recent illness, she probably wouldn't drink more than a sip of the champagne, but it was the principle.

Her car wasn't in the garage. Surely Miranda wouldn't have her working late on her first day back after being so sick. He brought in the champagne and the ingredients for dinner, and dialed Piper's number. No answer. A prickle of worry swept over him.

Spying a box in the living room floor, he relaxed. Of course. At the first sign of being human again, she'd headed over to her house to keep packing stuff. She'd probably set her phone down somewhere and didn't hear it. God forbid she wait until she was actually well.

Making a mental note to suck it up and hire

movers to pack everything for her, cost be damned, he went to put the chicken on to marinate and toss a couple of baked potatoes in the oven. They'd grill out, and he'd make her something with more taste than the bland soup and applesauce she'd been existing on the past week. Something niggled at him as he worked, but he couldn't put his finger on what was off.

As the clock ticked closer to six and she still hadn't shown, Myles figured he'd best head over to her place to remind her of the time. She'd work herself to collapse if he didn't. Keys in hand, he was almost out the door, when he turned back to the living room. Walking back in, he made a slow circle of the room.

Some of her stuff was gone. The stack of romance novels she kept by her end of the sofa wasn't on the end table. The bright pillows weren't on the couch. Had she moved them?

Feeling stupid and paranoid, he checked the rest of the house. She'd just picked up some. Maybe when she came home for her own lunch. But he didn't find the pillows, and the books weren't on the bookcase they'd hauled into the guest room.

Paranoia shifted to unease as he hit their bedroom. It was too…neat. Moving quicker now, he stepped into their closet—and found her half all but empty.

What the hell?

He was already racing for the door as he called her again. "C'mon. Pick up, woman!" As before, there was no answer.

Cursing, he tossed his phone into the cup holder and drove like a bat out of hell across town to her house. True worry set in when her car wasn't in the driveway.

"Where the hell are you, Piper?"

Myles didn't know what this meant, but it couldn't be anything good.

Checking his panic, he blew out a breath and called Tyler.

"Is Piper with you?" The question spilled out almost before she managed to say "Hello."

"No. I just got home from work. Why?"

"She should've been home from work by now. I thought she was packing, but I'm at her place, and she's not here either. I'm worried."

"I'm sure she's fine. Maybe she hit up Mc-Sweeney's for groceries or stopped by the pharmacy to pick up something."

But she wouldn't take her clothes to either of those places. He stopped himself from saying that. Saying it would make it real, and he wasn't ready to accept what his mind was already telling him.

"I'm sure you're right. If you hear from her, just...let me know, okay?"

"Sure."

Back in the car, he headed into town to drive by the grocery and pharmacy, just in case. He called Norah and had almost the same conversation.

He didn't have Miranda's number and didn't think to ask Norah for it, so he bypassed the phone entirely and drove to her house. One of the benefits of living in a small town. Her SUV was in the drive, engine still popping and cooling. She hadn't been home long. The door swung open before he could knock.

"Myles. What are you doing here?"

"Where is she?"

"Piper? I don't know. I haven't seen her since first thing this morning."

"She left work early?" Well, obviously she had. Patty had said she'd been by *The Observer*. He'd just assumed she'd gone back to work.

Miranda frowned. "Yeah, she was only in for about half an hour before I sent her home."

"Was she sick again? I told her she wasn't up to going back yet, but I'd have had to tie her down to keep her in bed another day." It was inane, normal conversation in the face of the panic working its way through him.

"She's never been a good patient." Miranda stepped back. "Why don't you come inside?"

Myles moved past her into the foyer. "What's going on?"

"She didn't come talk to you? Didn't call?"

"No. About what?"

"You really need to hear it from her."

He felt his head go light, a million awful possibilities spinning through his head. His hands were wrapped around her arms before he realized it. "Miranda, what's wrong with Piper?"

She hesitated, then shook her head. "As her doctor, I'm bound by confidentiality."

"I'm her husband."

"Unfortunately, that doesn't matter. You've never been put on the release form, so I can't tell you anything." She pulled away from him.

"What about as her friend?"

"As her friend, I'm telling you, you need to talk to your wife."

"She's gone." His voice cracked on the words. He scrubbed both hands over his hair, his face, as if that would somehow erase the harsh reality. "Her clothes are packed and she's not at her place."

Miranda's face twisted in sympathy. "Oh, Piper, what are you doing?"

"Just...just tell me. Is she sick? Cancer?

Some kind of autoimmune thing? Is she dying?" His throat closed up at the thought. She'd been so tired the last couple of weeks, and he'd barely been around to notice. What if it was something serious? They'd barely had any time together. How could he lose her now?

Miranda laid both hands on his shoulder. "I can't give you the specifics. But I don't think it's breaking any laws to tell you she's absolutely not dying."

"Then what the hell is going on?"

"I don't know."

"She's not answering her phone."

"Okay, sit down. Let me call and we'll at least establish whether she's avoiding you or if she's avoiding everyone."

Which of those options was supposed to be better?

Myles was far too agitated to sit. He paced the living room while Miranda made her attempt and got voicemail.

"Hey, sweetie. I was just calling to check on

you. Call me back, okay?" She hung up. "Not just you."

"Now what?"

"Honestly? The only thing you can do is wait. There's no reason to believe she's in any danger and not enough time has passed to file a missing persons report. You can check with her parents or Leah, but I doubt she'd go to them if she were upset."

Myles jerked toward her. "Upset? Why is she upset?"

Miranda spread her hands. "I'm making an assumption here. She wouldn't pack if she wasn't upset. It's the kind of impulsive thing she does. Did you two have a fight?"

"No. We've barely seen each other to fight. I was around more the last week while she was sick than I have been the entire time since we got back from our honeymoon. Work's been keeping me busy. I've been trying to move some things around and get things in place so that's not the case all the time."

And what the hell good was any of it if she'd left him?

"At this point, I think you should just go home and wait. Text her that you're worried. I'll get up with everyone else. If anybody hears from her, you'll be the first we notify, okay?"

"Okay." He let her shuffle him out of the house, climbed back into his car. But it wasn't okay. If she'd really left him, he wasn't sure it would ever be okay again.

He pulled out his phone and texted her. **Piper, I'm worried to death. Please just let me know you're safe.**

Myles stared at the screen, but there was no notice that the message had been read. No dancing bubbles to indicate a reply. Just silence. Terrifying silence.

He put the car into gear and began to drive. There was no way in hell he could just go home.

"I NEED YOUR GUEST ROOM."

Tucker took her overnight bag without question, and Piper was grateful. She needed all her flagging energy to make it up the stairs to his apartment. Her house would've been more practical, but that's the first place Myles would look, and she simply couldn't face him yet.

"You get your paperwork delivered?" he asked.

"Yes."

"Are you going to actually talk to me now?"

She didn't really want to talk to anybody. She wanted to go back to bed and wake up to find this was all a bad dream. But it wasn't a dream and, like it or not, she had to figure out what came next. And at least Tucker knew the truth about why she and Myles had married in the first place.

"Let me change first."

By the time she'd shed her suit in the name of pajamas, he'd put together a tray of cheese and crackers and poured a glass of wine.

"I figured you hadn't eaten."

"Food and I haven't exactly been on speaking terms for the last week." She picked up a cracker and nibbled. It immediately turned to ash on her tongue. Ignoring the wine, she moved into his galley style kitchen herself and poured a glass of water. She swallowed it down and filled the glass again, taking it back to the sofa. Tucker waited, expectant, a deceptively lazy slouch to his posture where he leaned against the bar.

"Oh, sit down. You're looming. Those courtroom intimidation tactics aren't going to work on me."

He crossed to a chair and sat, reaching for her hand. "What's going on, Pip?"

She swallowed against the sudden lump in her throat. The tears had been threatening all day, but she'd forced them down. Now, in the face of Tucker's support, she couldn't hold back the tide. "There is a distinct possibility I've completely fucked up my life." Her voice broke.

Tucker's eyes narrowed. "What did he do?"

"Don't. Don't go all brute squad on him.

This is my fault. My idea, my plan, my stupid, stupid heart."

"Tell me."

So she did. Letting the whole, horrible story spill out, including Suzanne's accusation of pregnancy on the news of their engagement and what Myles had said about why he wanted to marry her. The sympathy in his expression undid her, adding a soundtrack of tears as an underscore to the tale.

When she'd finished, he handed her a box of tissues. "I was afraid of something like this. And I'm sorry. I'm so sorry it didn't work out the way you wanted. But divorce—if that's actually what he meant by what he said—isn't the end of the world. It hurts, but you'd survive it. It's not going to ruin your life."

"Tucker, I'm pregnant."

His mouth fell open.

"I shouldn't be. I'm on birth control, and I used it exactly as intended. But there's always that one percent," she said bitterly. "When I came up with this whole crazy plan, it was supposed to be no big deal. No one was supposed to know we were married and we were just supposed to date like normal people. I wasn't supposed to fall in love with him, and I sure as hell wasn't supposed to get pregnant. Apparently, the Universe really wants to kick me in the ass to make sure I don't engage in any other crazy plans ever again."

"What did Myles say?"

"He doesn't know. That's why I went to his office this morning. To tell him. And after I overheard what he said, I didn't stick around."

"Piper, you have to tell him."

"How can I? Knowing he wants out, how can I tell him we've managed to complicate the hell out of that, too?"

"Better if he hears it first from you than in the middle of divorce proceedings." Tucker paused, his face going carefully blank. "Unless you don't intend to keep the pregnancy."

Piper's hand instinctively went to her still flat stomach. "I could never abort. It may not stick. Almost fifty percent of pregnancies don't before the end of the first trimester. But I'd never end it deliberately."

"Then you have to tell him. Sooner rather than later. You never know, it might change things. He's absolutely smitten with Preston."

This was the undeniable truth. Myles seemed to love children. But how could she endure a marriage where the love was for the child, not for her?

"No. I'm not going to stay in a loveless marriage for the sake of a child. I'm not. It isn't healthy for anybody involved."

"Sweetie, what if you're wrong? I don't think he'd have gone through everything he did with the wedding if he didn't love you on some level. What you heard might not even have been about you."

Piper fixed him with a glare. "Really? What the hell other extreme thing has he done in the name of the paper besides marrying me?"

"I don't know," Tucker said evenly. "And neither do you. Because you haven't talked to him."

A tiny ember of hope lit inside her. Could she be wrong?

No. He didn't love her. Didn't want to be with her. What was it he'd said? She wasn't who he thought she was. Why else would he have suddenly turned into a complete workaholic, keeping hours where he barely saw her at all, the moment they returned from their honeymoon?

Someone rang the doorbell, an insistent peal of bell.

"That'll be Myles."

"Did you call him?" Piper demanded.

"No. But by now he's realized you're gone. In his shoes, I'd be going all over town to every one of your friends trying to track you down."

"I can't face him yet, Tucker. Please."

He sighed. "Fine. I'll give you tonight. But you have to talk to him tomorrow."

Tucker left the door to downstairs open as he went to answer the door.

Piper rose to follow, pressing herself against the wall and out of sight.

"You look like shit," Tucker said.

"Is she here?" Myles sounded...rattled.

"Yes."

Myles' breath wheezed out. "Thank God."

He must've tried to push past and come up because Tucker said, "She doesn't want to see you."

"I need to talk to her."

"And she needs to talk to you. But it's not happening tonight. Go home. Give her some space."

"You really think I can just go home and wait this out? I don't even know what the hell is wrong. How can I fix it if she won't talk to me?"

What was there to fix? He was the one who wanted out.

"Look, she's here, she's safe. Right now, that's all you absolutely need to know. Just let her be."

"Tucker." Frustration and pleading filled every syllable.

"She'll come to you when she's ready."

Myles' sigh was heavy enough that she

heard it from the top of the stairs. "Okay. Just...take care of her."

"Always have."

"Thank you."

A minute later, the door shut and Tucker came back upstairs. His face was grave. "That was not a man who looked ready to divorce his wife. He was just about crazed with worry."

A trickle of guilt worked its way through the rest of her anxiety. "He's not a bad guy. I should've let him know I was okay. Or at least that I wasn't dead in a ditch somewhere."

It hadn't even occurred to her to turn her phone back on.

"Look, this is obviously your decision, but as your friend, as your legal counsel, I'm telling you to talk to your husband. Find out for sure what's going on. I'm positive there's more to this than you think."

Piper didn't dare consider that possibility. How much worse would it be to foolishly give flight to hope, only to have everything dashed yet again when it turned out everything was exactly as she thought? But he was right. She did need to talk to Myles.

"Fine. But tomorrow. Right now, I just want to try to sleep. I'm exhausted, and I feel like absolute crap."

"I'll make up the guest bed for you."

"MR. BONDURANT IS HERE."

Myles looked up at Patty, not really seeing her. "Okay."

She stepped into his office. "Jesus Christ, Myles, are you really meeting with the man like that?"

Wearing the same rumpled clothes from yesterday because he'd been up here all night replaying every moment of his relationship with Piper, trying to sort out where he'd gone wrong? Unshowered, unshaved? "Yep."

Bondurant ought to consider himself lucky

Myles wasn't drunker than Cooter Brown. The urge to drown his sorrows in the scotch hanging out in his bottom desk drawer had been strong. But on the off chance that Piper decided she was ready to talk, he needed to be capable of driving.

Patty shut the door and crossed over, laying a hand on his brow in a universal maternal thermometer. "What's wrong?"

The woman I love has left me, and I don't know why. I find I don't really give a rat's ass about anything else.

"Did you and Piper have a fight?"

"No." He'd never even been given the chance to fight. Or maybe he'd been too wrapped up in the paper for her to even bother.

Not wanting to answer any more questions, he shoved back from his desk.

"Hold it." Patty opened a file cabinet drawer and pulled out an emergency shirt. "At least put this on so you look a little less like a vagrant."

"I have the check. I don't give a damn if I

look homeless when I give it to him. I just want this over with."

Leaving her gaping, Myles strode down the hall to the conference room.

Bondurant stood at the window, his briefcase at one end of the table, neatly squared with the edges. The other man turned as Myles came in. "Good Lord."

"Mr. Bondurant."

"Are you...all right?"

"Most assuredly not. I would appreciate it if we could get this show on the road. I have more important things to deal with."

"I'm afraid there's a slight delay."

"Delay?" Myles growled.

"Your investor has decided to meet with you in person to conclude the transaction."

That caught his wandering attention. All their dealings had been done through Bondurant's firm as a proxy. At no point had Myles even met his investor. The name on all the contracts was the business manager of the corporation. The rigid confidentiality surrounding the deal had bothered him, but none of his digging had uncovered anything unscrupulous, so he'd let it go.

"Why now?"

"I'm afraid that's not for me to say."

Impatience snapped through him like a dog on a chain. "This better not be some attempt to renegotiate terms. I have the full amount for the payoff. I want to be free of this debt."

"And you will be once we're finished here."

Surprise had him swinging around. "Gram? What the hell are you doing here?"

"Is that any way to greet your grandmother?" She stalked into the room, and he wondered what she had to be pissed off about. Her life wasn't falling apart.

Then Myles saw his dad lingering in the hallway. When he didn't follow her inside, Gram did an about face and actually grabbed him by the ear to drag him into the room.

"*Mother.*" He pulled free, rubbing at his reddened ear.

"Hush it. It's your fault we're in this mess," Gram snapped.

Myles glanced from one to the other, then back to Mr. Bondurant, who just seemed embarrassed by the whole proceeding. "Look, I don't know what's going on here, but I'm in the middle of a business meeting."

"Yes. Paying off your investor." She swung toward Warrick, arms crossed. "Tell him."

"Tell me what?" Myles ground out.

His father didn't meet his eyes, looking at Mr. Bondurant instead. "You have the final paperwork, John?"

"Of course, Mr. Stewart." The briefcase opened with a decisive snick.

Myles stared, his sleep-deprived brain refusing to accept what was obviously going on. "You? You were my investor?"

"Yes."

"I'm sorry, did the Devil get snowed in and I missed it?"

Warrick sighed. "Given the contention between us, it seemed simpler all around to conduct the transaction via proxies through my shell companies."

Myles' world had already been off its axis since Piper left. This just broke his entire world view. His father, the man who'd done every damned thing to try to lure, bully, and drag Myles into the family business, had actually invested in his dream?

"Why would you invest in the paper? You've always despised the fact that I went into journalism."

"I saw an opportunity to help you get this newspaper thing out of your system so you could get back on track."

"On track?"

"Yes. I figured you'd have a good shot, learn that there's no future in this business and would come home with a clear conscience."

Myles' temper rose as his world tipped back into recognizable territory. "So you pulled funding early, thinking I'd just capitulate."

"Well, that was the original plan, but then

you pulled this whole trust fund wedding stunt and that impressed me."

"Honestly, Warrick!" Gram snapped, disgust evident in every line of her face.

"That *impressed* you?" Myles demanded.

"Yes. I didn't expect you to go after the trust. It was set up so long ago, I'd forgotten about it. But that kind of Hail Mary shows that this isn't some lark or experiment you'll drop when things get hard. It shows how dedicated you are to making this paper work. It shows grit I didn't know you had."

"Grit," Myles repeated.

"Absolutely," Warrick said, with more enthusiasm. "The whole thing made me really look at what you were doing here for the first time. And I realized, you've really got something here, son. Against all the current trends and dire forecasts about the newspaper business, you're turning this paper around. I even thought about calling it off, leaving my investment in place, despite the fact that you don't need me anymore."

His whole life, Myles had wanted his father's approval. The gravity of it settled over him, making him feel like his dad finally saw him as an adult for the first time. The unexpected validation of his life's dream was sweet, and his immediate instinct was to tell Piper. She'd understand what this meant to him. But the ache at not being able to tell her, at maybe never getting that chance, left him with an aching void in his chest. If the cost of all this was losing her, he didn't want it.

"I went into this on good faith, thinking the investment was legitimate. I worked my ass off building this, and all this time, I was building a house of cards on a rug you were just waiting to pull out from under me."

Warrick's eyes widened. "That's not—"

"You backed me into a corner. I was on a good trajectory with the revitalization of the paper before you sent me into a tailspin. If you hadn't interfered, Piper and I would have dated like normal people, fallen in love like normal people, gotten married like normal people, after a normal amount of time to build a proper foundation. And instead, because of your Machiavellian scheming, we rushed things to try to save my business, and now I've *lost my wife*."

"Now hold it," Gram interrupted. "That's not all on Warrick. Yes, he was wrong and yes, it was his manipulation that prompted such a desperate act. But however much you felt backed into a corner, you still made the choice to marry for money, and Piper assured me that she was the instigator of the whole thing."

Myles froze.

"Oh yes, Piper told me everything."

"When?" he demanded.

"Yesterday. When she came to bring me this." Gram removed an envelope from her purse and slid it across the table.

Myles picked it up, dread a festering knot in his gut. Unfolding the papers, he read them over, the knot drawing tighter with every word. A post-nuptial agreement, relinquishing any and all rights to the assets he brought to the marriage via trust, family ties, or otherwise.

"I will take responsibility for her feeling the need to do this in the first place, but I place the blame for the rest squarely on you."

"The rest?"

"What the hell is wrong with you?"

"What the hell is wrong with me?" Myles demanded. "Dad's the one who backed me into a goddamned corner in the first place!"

Gram ignored his rage and reached up to cup his cheek. "If you were that desperate, why didn't you come to me?"

Myles only stared at her, thrown by the uncharacteristically maternal gesture. Come to her? Why on earth would he have come to her?

"Even if I couldn't give you access to the trust, you could've made a case for a personal loan from me, against the trust."

Had he ever seen her like this, with the mask of family matriarch askew enough to suggest a softer side? Maybe when he'd been a child. But not in years. Bemused at the change, he almost smiled. "That's…that never occurred to me." He assumed his grandmother would take the same dismissive attitude toward his dreams as his father always had.

"That's because you're a fool." She gave his chin a none-too-gentle tweak.

And we're back.

Myles rubbed a hand over his stubbly chin. "Would you have done it?"

"Honestly, I don't know. It's in the past. Because even though you married to gain access to the trust, from the moment you said your I dos, the paper and all the financial strain that goes with it were no longer the important thing. Piper is the important thing. And she has no idea."

"How? *How* can she not know she's the most important thing in my life?"

"What did you expect, Myles? You spent all that effort and charm on her up through the wedding. What on earth did you do when you got back to make her think you don't love her?"

Because I haven't told her. Because I'm a fucking

dumbass.

"That poor girl sat in the parlor barely holding it together, putting on a brave face and acting like it was just a business arrangement that was finished."

He jerked to a stop. "What did you say?"

"She was upset—"

"No, the other thing. Business arrangement. What were the exact words she used?"

"She said that it was just business."

The blood drained out of his head. "Oh God. Patty said Piper was in the office yesterday morning, but I never saw her. She must have overheard me talking about Vanessa with Simone and thought I was talking about her."

"Who's Vanessa?"

"The new assistant editor I just hired so that I can stop working every waking hour of the day and spend time with my wife. The assistant editor I hadn't told her about because it was meant to be a surprise."

"So you said not a word about any of that, and you came home and reverted to your workaholic ways in order to pull it off," Gram surmised. "Leaving your new wife with nothing else to think but that you really were in it only for the paper."

If that's what she believed, no wonder she'd left him.

"I have to talk to her. I have to fix this."

"You have to prove to her that you've always been in this for her. Your father may have manipulated you into acting, but you'd never have gone through with the marriage if you didn't love her. It's not how you're built. And she wouldn't have suggested it if she didn't love you."

There was still hope, if he could only get her to listen. But he couldn't get through Tucker, so how was he going to even get in the same room with her? He considered the only thing that might pull her out of hiding. It was sneaky and manipulative in its own right, but desperate times called for desperate measures.

Pulling out his phone, he dialed his sister-in-law. "Leah, it's Myles. I need your help."

I AM A COWARD, Piper thought as she pulled into Leah's driveway.

She should've gone home and waited for Myles. She'd promised Tucker she'd talk to him today. She'd even taken another day off work to wallow in her self-pity and psych herself up for the confrontation. Now that the worry had passed, how would he react? Anger? Frustration? Relief? He'd all but turned the town upside down looking for her last night, practically beating down the doors of all her friends to find her. Piper couldn't reconcile that with what she'd overheard. But she was too afraid to hope she was wrong. And she was terrified of getting confirmation that she was right. So when her sister had texted in need of an emergency babysitter, she'd jumped at the chance. Having some quality one-on-one time with her nephew might be the lone bright spot to what would undoubtedly be a horrible day.

Besides, if Myles was true to form, he wouldn't even be off work yet.

Piper let herself in, calling out over the recognizable sounds of Blues Clues, "Leah?"

Preston, who'd been playing with trucks in front of the TV, leapt up, making a beeline for Piper with a screech of glee. "Pie!"

She scooped him up, feeling her heart squeeze with gratitude for this tiny boy who never failed to lighten her mood. Pressing a smacking kiss to his sticky mouth, she said, "You know what the absolute best thing about you is, Pres?"

He angled his head, waiting.

"You love me for me, exactly as I am." She cuddled him close, loving the feel of his little arms wrapped tight around her neck.

Leah appeared in the hallway. "The rest of us love you for exactly who you are, too."

Piper bridled. She couldn't help it. The reaction was so long ingrained, it rose up and spilled out before she could stop it. "You have to say that. You're my sister."

But for once, Leah didn't rise to the bait. "Sweetie, I know you think you're the black sheep of the family, and maybe there's some truth to that. You aren't like the rest of us, and that means a lot of times we don't understand you. But that's never meant we don't love you."

"I know you love me."

"Do you? Do you really know that?"

"Sure. In an *if I needed a kidney and one of you was a match, I know you wouldn't hesitate to give it* kind of way."

Her sister blew out a breath. "Come back and talk to me while I finish my makeup."

Piper really didn't feel like discussing this, but she'd inadvertently opened this can of worms. She could deal with listening to why Leah thought she was wrong. Again.

"You want to hang in here with Blue?" Piper asked Preston.

"MyPie!"

Piper closed her eyes, a part of her weeping for the fact that her nephew was just as in love with Myles as she was. How could she break his heart too?

"No Uncle Myles tonight, buddy boy."

He wiggled to be let down and went racing down the hall to his room. "MyPie!"

She'd go play with him once Leah was gone.

Her sister stood at the bathroom vanity, smoothing foundation over her face. "I've been thinking about this a lot since that day we went dress shopping."

Piper had been trying to put that fight out of her mind. "Oh?"

"I was really upset by what you said."

Ugh, not this again. "I wasn't trying to hurt you—"

"I know. You didn't even know I was there, and that made you more candid than you might otherwise have been. Which is saying something. But I wasn't hurt because you were angry —at least not much. I was hurt because you truly seem to believe that we expect you to change."

Because every sigh, every wince, every baffled

shake of head says exactly that. But Leah seemed to legitimately be trying to say something here, so Piper kept that to herself.

Leah swept blush along the high cheekbones that matched Piper's own. "Do you know why Mom and I got so excited about your wedding?"

"Because good Southern girls get married."

Leah rolled her eyes and proceeded to swipe on mascara. "Because it was finally something we both felt like we could relate to you about. We've spent all your life trying to find common ground and failing."

Of course, she'd managed to screw that up, too. What would they say when she turned up divorced and pregnant?

Black sheep to the end.

"You aren't anything like us. And that's *fine.* It doesn't mean we love or appreciate you any less."

"I'm pretty sure Mom would appreciate it fine if I learned to hold my tongue and got my give-a-damn switch fixed."

Lips twitching, Leah met her eyes in the mirror. "That may be true. Mom's old school. But the fact that you're gutsy and don't care what other people think? That's one of the things I love most about you. I don't know how to do that. I've got this gigantic filter between my brain and my mouth and I almost never get to say exactly what I think because I'm too worried about how somebody would take it, and what if they're offended or don't like me anymore."

"I find that kind of thinking exhausting. Which is why I don't bother with it."

"I love that about you." She flashed a rueful smile. "I don't always like what you're saying, but the fact that you're fearless enough to say it? I admire the heck out of that. I always have. You're brave."

Piper thought of the confrontation awaiting her. The one she'd keep avoiding if she could. "I'm not brave."

"But you are. You get out there and do things. You make a difference. You get up there on stage and put yourself out there in front of an actual audience, and you're great at it. I could never do that. I'm terrified of even the idea of doing something in front of an audience."

"What do you call attending a Junior Auxiliary meeting?"

Leah laughed. "Synchronized gossip."

"I call it hell."

"Fair enough. Though if you came, those meetings would be a lot more entertaining."

"They'd toss me out in five minutes and you know it."

"I'm pretty sure the scandalized look on Becky Palmer's face would be worth it." Leah's mouth twitched into a wicked grin that had Piper's own smile flickering.

Leah turned from the mirror and gripped Piper by the arms. "We love you. And we've got your back, no matter what."

Was there something else behind that declaration? Did she know what was going on with Myles?

No. She'd never be able to resist interfering if she knew.

Still, Piper appreciated the show of support. She pulled Leah into a hug. "Thanks. I really needed to hear that today."

Leah pulled back and framed her face. "You're looking a little peaked, sis. You feeling okay?"

Not even a little bit. But that was a topic she didn't have any intention of discussing with her sister. "Aren't you going to be late?"

She checked her watch. "Oh crap, you're right. I'm not sure how long I'll be. A couple hours at least. Elliott's out of town for a work thing, so I really appreciate you pinch hitting for me."

"No problem."

"I'm sneaking out before Preston realizes I'm leaving. Thank you!"

And then she was gone, leaving Piper alone with her thoughts and the two-year-old she was relying on to distract her.

Preston was being way too quiet. Always an

ominous sign with a toddler. He'd either fallen asleep or was getting into trouble. Heading back to his room, Piper heard him happily babbling to himself. Not asleep then.

She pushed the door open. "Who you talking to, Pres?"

His little face brightened and he clapped his hands. "MyPie!"

A figure unfolded from the chair in the corner. "Piper."

Myles had crossed the room, tugging her roughly into his arms almost before she finished her *eep* of surprise. He held her tightly, his face buried in her hair, and all she wanted to do was burrow in and cry.

"Don't." The word came out sharper than she intended, as much a reminder to herself as an order to him.

He stiffened and let his arms drop.

Because she didn't trust herself, Piper scooted out of his reach, moving to scoop up Preston.

Using the toddler as a shield. Real brave move there.

But maybe with the child between them, it would keep the harsh words to a minimum. For now, at least.

Myles stood where she'd left him beside the bedroom door. Now that she got a good look at him, she could see the two-day growth of beard and the shadows around his eyes. His cheeks stood out in sharp relief and the nurse in her couldn't resist asking, "Are you feeling all right?"

"I'm not ill, if that's what you mean. I didn't sleep last night. I was too busy wracking my brain, trying to figure out why you've reverted to the role of Betty Haynes."

"Excuse me?" Whatever she'd expected him to say, it wasn't that.

"Did you think I wouldn't recognize it after spending months watching you play it in *White Christmas*? I know you better than that."

"What are you talking about?"

"She found out something that upset her, and instead of staying and dealing with it, she ran all the way to the Carousel Club in New York. You did the same thing, except instead of me catching up with you at the train station and at least getting a half-as—" He shot a glance at Preston. "—half-baked explanation, you moved out. Without a word. I mean, I guess I've been playing Bob, the clueless schmuck, so maybe it fits. But you had me worried sick about you, Piper."

"Why?"

He stared at her. "Why was I worried sick when I came home to find *my wife* had apparently left me? Why do you think?"

To protect your investment. The words clogged in her throat. "I want to hear you say it."

"Why on Earth should I have to state the obvious? Haven't I made it clear?" His voice was full of annoyed frustration.

But he hadn't made it clear. Not truly. And if she was going to walk away, she needed to know for certain, or she'd wonder for the rest of her life. "I need the words, Myles."

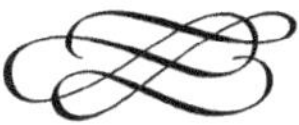

CHAPTER 17

*S*HE DOESN'T KNOW.

THE realization slammed into Myles as he took in sight of her clutching the child, shoulders hunched against an expected a blow, an expression of resignation and dread on her face. Gram had said as much, but he hadn't believed her. After everything he'd done, he hadn't thought it possible that Piper didn't know that he loved her.

She must've been squeezing Preston too tight. He began to squirm, little arms shoving at her to let him go. Piper's face spasmed at that, as if that rejection was too much. But she set him on the floor, where he went back to his Duplo blocks.

Myles stepped around the pile of blocks and reached for her, trying to ignore the whip of pain at her flinch. "Piper, I was worried because I love you."

Her gaze flew to his, the surprise there making him want to curse.

"I love you," he repeated, more forcefully, framing her face in his hands.

But she didn't relax, didn't lean into him. Her eyes swam with unshed tears and her voice was a ragged whisper. "But not enough."

"What?"

"You love the idea of me. The role. Some modern version of Betty Haynes or June Cleaver, who has a ready smile and a warm dinner waiting whenever you deign to come home from work, just like my mother said. I guess I can't blame you for that. What guy wouldn't want that? But I can't maintain that. And you'd already figured that out. You said it yourself. I'm not who you thought I was, and you've got nothing more to give. I heard you talking to Simone. And I'm not going to fight you about cutting me loose. We had a business arrangement, and it's not your fault I forgot that."

Disbelief was the only thing keeping him silent long enough for her to finish. If this was what she believed, no wonder she'd moved out. No wonder she looked like he'd kicked her. A part of him wanted to rage that she could think this of him, but that would accomplish nothing. The record had to be set straight.

"Do you know what the first rule of journalism is? Always verify the facts."

A guarded hope sprang into her eyes, but she said nothing.

"Fact: Yes, I'm a guy, so coming home to a hot meal and a smile and a warm, willing wife is a pretty freaking awesome way to end the day. But I certainly don't expect it of you if you don't feel like it. You're human. You have crappy days, like anybody else, and sometimes you're the one who needs the hot meals and a smile and a blanket fort. I've fallen down on that the last few weeks, but it doesn't mean I don't know it. I don't expect you to be June Cleaver. That's not who you are. And I can only assume your mother gets credit for shoving that particular brand of BS in your head."

She opened her mouth to say something, but Myles just shook his head. "I'm not finished yet. Fact: What you heard me talking to Simone about was the new assistant editor I just hired. Vanessa was playing hardball and had just sent back a counter offer I couldn't meet. I had decided to rescind the offer rather than keep playing that game. She was the one I was planning to cut loose. That deal is part of what's kept me so busy lately. I've been trying to find the right person to bring in so that I can legitimately hand off some responsibility of the paper. Because I don't want to work sixteen-hour days when you're there to come home to. And as it turns out, when I cut the crap and told

Vanessa that, it was a decision she could respect. She starts next month."

"You...hired help to free up time...for me?"

Myles curled his hands around her arms and shook her, just a little. "*Yes.* And here's another fact: This was never a business arrangement. Getting access to the trust to save my business was a component, but I married you because I wanted to, because you're fun and smart and sexy. I married you because I want a life with you, and when you were crazy enough to be willing to marry me, I wasn't about to miss the chance. I want a future with you. Kids. A sloppy dog. Rocking chairs on the front porch when we're eighty. The whole shebang. I want *you*, Piper. Exactly as you are. And I will fight tooth and nail to keep you because I love you more than I imagined possible. I don't know how you didn't know that."

The tears spilled over and gutted him. "You never said it."

"I did everything I knew how to show you."

A flash of consternation showed through

the tears. "You're a *journalist*. How can you, of all people, not know the power of words?"

"Because I'm a journalist I know how easy it is to spin words, to twist them to say something you don't really mean. Hell, I didn't even learn that from journalism. I learned it at home, from my own family. Words are cheap. Nobody knows that better than someone who spends eons choosing the right one for the right impact."

Her throat worked. "They aren't cheap to me."

"Then I'll splash it on the front page. I'll make a special section for it in every edition. I'll hire a skywriter, if that's what you need. Just… don't walk away."

She gave a watery laugh. "I don't need public declarations. I just…need to hear it."

Myles pulled her into his arms, his own heart starting to beat again as she wrapped hers around him. He pressed his brow to hers. "I love you. And I'll say it every day for the rest of our lives."

"I can live with that."

PIPER SIGHED, the tension of the last couple of days draining away. Weak and giddy with relief, she absorbed the warmth of Myles' arms around her, the soft woosh of his breath inches away.

He loved her.

She'd been so very, very wrong. Thank God.

And now that her world had been set to rights, she needed to rock his one more time.

Before she could open her mouth to speak, a crash sounded from the kitchen.

Piper's gaze shot to the blocks, but of course her nephew hadn't sat around while they'd been intent on saving their marriage. She bolted into the kitchen, Myles on her heels, then skidded to a stop at the edge of the disaster.

"I don't think we'll be getting our bread this week," Myles observed.

Preston had somehow turned over the

twenty-five-pound bucket of flour Leah kept by the counter, dumping the contents all over the kitchen floor, splashing it up on the cabinets and all over himself. A fog of it hung in the air. But that hadn't been the source of the crash.

He'd dragged in the stool that usually lived in the bathroom so he could get to the faucet to wash his hands. The little monkey had used it to get to the kitchen sink to fill a little bucket, the kind more appropriate for a beach vacation. It was currently overflowing—thankfully still in the sink—from the still running tap. Judging by the spreading mess of wet, he'd managed to dump at least a couple of buckets on the flour already. A sand spade was stuck in the middle, coated with glop.

Preston himself perched on the edge of the counter, looking down at where his stool had been knocked over. Seeing the two of them standing in the doorway, he reached his arms out. "Down."

Caught somewhere between horror and

amusement, Piper choked out, "Well, at least he's not bleeding."

"What are you doing, little monkey?" Myles asked, skirting the edge of the mess to pluck him, sticky hands and all, off the counter.

"Sand castle." He wiggled to get down, but Myles held firm.

"That, my fine fellow, is not sand. And you have made quite the mess."

Preston shot him a flour streaked grin.

Her husband shook his head. "Well, I do recall saying you'd be good practice."

Piper's lips twitched. He had no idea how accurate that statement was. "And what lesson have we learned?"

"That it takes less than three minutes for a toddler to get into things if you aren't paying attention?"

"File that one away. As they get more mobile, the span shortens." Was now the moment? In the middle of this toddler-authored chaos? Probably not the best time, even if Myles looked more amused that distressed. She moved over and tweaked her nephew's nose. "We need to get this cleaned up before your mommy gets home and bans us from babysitting duty. Divide and conquer. Take him on into the bath. I'll get started on this."

"You sure? Seems like you're getting the bigger job here." He had streaks of flour on his face from Preston's grabby little hands.

She was definitely getting the better end of this stick. "I know where all the cleaning supplies are. Just...keep him wrangled long enough for me to use them."

So Myles hauled Preston back to the bathroom, keeping him entertained with what sounded like an epic battle of rubber duckies versus the cast of *Little Nemo*, while she cleaned up the mess. The mindless domesticity settled her, giving her mind a chance to truly empty out from all the angst and heartache. By the time the kitchen was set to rights, she felt calmer and ready to drop her little bomb.

She leaned in the doorway to the bathroom, taking in this new scene of chaos. Wet towels were strewn across the floor and Preston's entire collection of bath toys floated around him in what couldn't have been more than a couple of inches of water. Myles perched on the closed lid of the toilet, rubber duckies in both hands as he talked some sort of nonsense to Preston. Her bruised heart swelled with warmth. He was going to be an amazing father.

"Did you leave any of the water in the actual tub?"

Myles looked up and she realized he'd cleaned his own face. "A bit. Pretty sure a fair bit wound up on me. My rubber duckie armada put up a valiant fight."

"So I see." Moving into the bathroom, she handed him the hooded frog towel hanging on a hook.

Myles scooped a giggling and clean Preston out of the bath and briskly rubbed him down. "Jammie time, boy-o."

Piper followed them into Preston's room, pulling out a fresh diaper and choo-choo train pajamas. Between the two of them, they managed to get him wrestled into them both.

"We've got this babysitting gig down. Good team." He lifted his hand to give her a high five.

But instead of slapping his palm, she placed her hand against his, lacing their fingers together. "Myles, there's something I need to tell you."

He frowned. "About the post nup? Gram already told me. We'll tear it up."

That was something else they should probably talk about at some point. God knew what his grandmother thought. But whatever needed to be faced with his family, they'd face together. Right now was just for them.

"Not the post-nup. It's why I was at your office at all yesterday."

Pure panic flashed in his expression and he tightened his grip, pulling her closer, his words spilling out in a rush. "Are you sick? Miranda wouldn't tell me what was wrong, just that it wasn't terminal. Whatever it is, we'll deal with it together, okay? We'll find all the best doctors. We'll—"

With a hint of a smile, Piper pressed a finger to his lips, stemming the flow. "I'm not sick. And I didn't have the stomach flu." She took a breath and blew it out in a rush. "I'm pregnant."

He blinked as if she'd koshed him over the head. "What?"

"We're having a baby."

More blinking. "But how?"

Piper couldn't stop the wicked smile remembering all those opportunities for the how. "The usual way. Apparently, I fall into that one percent of cases where birth control failed. I suppose you have really determined sperm."

"We made a baby? Really?" He was looking at her, but not really. Piper couldn't read him. Was this still shock or was he trying to hold back his reaction?

"Yeah." She bit her lip. "I'm sorry."

Myles attention suddenly focused laser sharp on her. "I'm not." His grin stretched wide, bursting across his face like a sunrise. "This is awesome!" He picked her up and spun her around with a whoop that had Preston giggling. "Did you hear that Pres? I'm gonna be a daddy! You're gonna get a cousin to corrupt."

"You're really happy?" God knew she couldn't trust her own interpretation of things just now.

"Are you kidding? A piece of you and a piece of me? How awesome is that?" He laid his free hand over her flat belly. "We're going to be a family." The soft reverence in his voice absolutely undid her.

Piper laid her hand over his, fighting tears again—happy ones this time. "I thought you'd be…well, honestly, I had no idea how you'd react. I've been freaking out."

"Why? You're going to make an amazing mother." His unshakable conviction bolstered her.

"We didn't plan on this. We haven't even talked about kids or a timeline—"

Myles cut her off with a lingering kiss. "Sweetheart, I think we just need to accept that we're never going to do anything on a normal timeline, ever."

She settled against him with a contented sigh. "You make a good point."

"And you know what?" He laced his hands at the small of her back. "I wouldn't have it any other way."

EPILOGUE

14 Months Later

Piper woke disoriented. Was it the baby? She listened with that part of her mother's brain that could assess in an instant whether she needed to get up, while keeping her eyes shut. If it was nothing, she'd slip back into blissful sleep. For at least five more minutes.

But she didn't hear Parker. She heard…birdsong?

Her eyes flew open to see daylight. Daylight? *What time is it?*

The bedside clock read 8:14. Dumbfounded,

she stared. That couldn't be right. Could it? She hadn't slept this late in months. Not since well before Parker was born. Hearing absolutely nothing in the house, she had a moment of irrational panic. Had everyone suddenly died in the night?

This is what the zombie apocalypse sounds like.

She rolled over. Myles wasn't in bed, but the newspaper was. On his pillow lay a copy of the Sunday edition, neatly folded so that his editorial was front and center. If the zombie apocalypse had hit, he wouldn't have left her reading material.

Propping herself up in bed, Piper picked it up and began to read.

The Wishful Observer
Sunday, June 18

The Things No One Told Me About Fatherhood

By Myles Stewart

Confession: Before this time last year, I'd never given much thought to being a father. Parenthood was one of those things that hung out on the horizon of the distant, hazy Someday. A Thing You Are Supposed To Do, but not one I'd given any serious consideration. At least not until I met my wife. Even then, with occasional daydreams of what traits our offspring might get from each of us, it was still a Thing of the Future.

The whole prospect became very real in the months following our wedding, while my wife valiantly struggled through what I am convinced was the worst case of morning sickness the world has ever known. (Editor's note: She informs me there is a condition known as hyperemesis gravidarum that is far worse. I shudder to imagine.) Either way, it's a horrible thing, to see the woman you love fighting a personal war against an enemy you can't see and not being able to do anything more than offer sympathies, cold washcloths, and endless supplies of ginger ale.

There are so many things I simply didn't know.

No one told me that finding out I was going to be a father would feel like winning the lottery.

No one told me that I'd be having lengthy conversations with my wife's swelling belly, already striving to teach my kid the important stuff in life, like the fact that, when it comes to *Star Wars*, nothing before Episode IV actually counts.

No one told me that quite a few of the injuries in the delivery room are from fathers passing out upon seeing the harsh, brutal reality of labor. I didn't *actually* do this, but it was a near thing. Men, there is a reason the Almighty did not see fit to saddle us with the responsibility of growing humans. Quite simply, we aren't strong enough. If the continuation of the human race fell to mankind alone, we'd never have survived this long. All of you take a knee for a minute and honor your mothers and the mothers of your children.

No one told me that seeing my daughter born would make my heart crack clean in two because it was growing three sizes, Grinch-style, in the span of one breath and the next, when I heard her cry for the first time.

No one told me I'd love her so much that I wouldn't even mind the fact that she's entirely a creature of the night and believes that sleeping is for wimps. Though, that could be the sleep deprivation talking. God makes babies cute to override our instincts for self-preservation because we'd never go through this for anything else.

No one told me she'd have the sweetest smile on earth and that I'd already be planning interrogation tactics for the boys who want to date her—who, of course, she won't be allowed to actually go out with until she's thirty.

No one told me that *I'd* be the one to cry when she started day care. You'll recognize her as the most beautiful little girl there, the precocious one with the shockingly full head of hair and the philosopher's eyes. Don't believe me? Spend five minutes staring into her eyes and see if you don't start contemplating the mysteries of the universe.

No one told me that parenthood would be the greatest adventure of my life or that each day would be full of more joy than I thought existed in the world.

Most of all, no one told me that I could actually feel even more for my wife than I did the day that I married her—which says a lot, because I flash-mobbed my own wedding just for her.

She and Parker are my greatest treasures. So rather than spending Father's Day being celebrated as a father, I'll celebrate the gift of being made one. I can't imagine anything greater.

P.S. Piper, I love you.

No matter how many editorials he wrote, she never got tired of seeing that post script. He used it on every single one, regardless of topic. But this one. This one made her feel gooey inside. He'd said once that he figured she'd be surprising him for the next fifty years. It seemed he planned to do the same for her.

Slipping out of bed, she went in search of her sweet husband. The reason for the silence became readily apparent once she hit the living room. Myles was fast asleep in his favorite chair, feet stretched out on the ottoman. Parker was snuggled up on his chest. Unlike her father, she was awake, her big blue eyes fixed in a staring contest with Loaf, the corgi mix they'd adopted from the shelter. As Piper watched,

Parker reached out a tiny hand and booped Loaf's nose.

Where is the camera when I need it?

The dog rose from a sit and nosed Parker's hand. She gave a happy burble and Myles jolted awake, his arms coming around her.

"How's my little cutie pie?" He pressed a kiss to Parker's downy head.

"Having a little daddy-daughter time?"

"You're up. Sleep okay?"

"I did. I feel almost like a real human." Piper crossed over to the chair, perching on the arm and leaning down to kiss him. "Although it's Father's Day. I should've been letting you sleep in."

"I have exactly what I want, right here. My two best girls."

"I read your editorial."

His eyes brightened. "Yeah? What did you think?"

"It was somewhat hyperbolic, but completely you. You undo me, Myles."

"Just speaking the truth."

When he tugged her into his lap, Piper fell willingly, snuggling them both. "I love you. However, you're still not changing my mind."

"Aw, come on," he pleaded. "Just look at her." He waved Parker's little arm and bounced his leg, making her giggle.

Piper held out a finger for her to grip. God, she was growing so fast. "Yes, she's the most adorable baby ever. And we're still not starting on a second one until she's at least two."

He mimed a pout that looked an awful lot like one of Parker's.

"Nice try. Not happening, my love. I've made sure of that."

"As I recall, you were pretty sure of it the last time, and we got the world's greatest oops out of the bargain." The grin he flashed held a wicked edge.

Piper looked to the heavens. "Please, dear God, cover your ears and don't listen to him."

"Party pooper."

"Yes, pooper! We already have two. Only one of them goes outside. That's enough for now. I will, however, make you some Father's Day pancakes."

Loaf barked in approval.

"Pancakes sound awesome."

As she moved into the kitchen, Myles followed, Parker on his hip and a faint frown on his face.

"You're really disappointed about this, aren't you?"

"A little, yeah. I mean, I know it's kind of crazy. But they say it can take a long time to get pregnant with the second one."

"Or it can happen in an instant. Case in point." She gave her daughter a smacking kiss. "Now turn that frown upside down and pack an overnight bag for Parker."

"Why?'"

"Because she's going to stay at Grandma's for the night so you can get the rest of your Father's Day present."

His eyes lit with interest. "Which is?"

"A night of completely uninterrupted sleep." She sent a saucy grin his way. "And maybe me in that negligee you got me for Valentine's that I haven't had a proper opportunity to wear."

One brow winged up. "Oh yeah?"

Piper winked. "I said we weren't having a second baby yet. I never said we couldn't practice."

Choose Your Next Romance!

Next up in the Wishful line up, we have a billionaire heiress in HIDING! Way back in *To Get Me To You,* Norah promised Cecily she'd introduce her to Cam's cousins. And she did. And Reed blew it. *Wish I Might* is the story of him figuring out how and earning a second chance. Fans of the Campbells will enjoy this look at the youngest of the bunch.

If you'd rather stick with the community theater crowd, then you'll want to dance on over to *Turn My World Around,* where Tucker gets drafted by Norah as a dancer in a local

Dancing With The Stars style fundraiser. And his partner is none other than former mean girl Corinne Dawson. This is a heartwarming, redemption romance that shows that we are more than the sum of our pasts.

A complete and up-to-date list of all my books can be found at https://kaitnolan.com.

THE MISFIT INN SERIES
SMALL TOWN FAMILY ROMANCE

- *When You Got A Good Thing* (Kennedy and Xander)
- *Til There Was You* (Misty and Denver)

- *Those Sweet Words* (Pru and Flynn)
- *Stay A Little Longer* (Athena and Logan)
- *Bring It On Home* (Maggie and Porter)

RESCUE MY HEART SERIES
SMALL TOWN MILITARY ROMANCE

- *Baby It's Cold Outside* (Ivy and Harrison)
- *What I Like About You* (Laurel and Sebastian)
- *Bad Case of Loving You* (Paisley and Ty prequel)
- *Made For Loving You* (Paisley and Ty)

MEN OF THE MISFIT INN
SMALL TOWN SOUTHERN ROMANCE

- *Let It Be Me* (Emerson and Caleb)
- *Our Kind of Love* (Abbey and Kyle)

WISHFUL SERIES

SMALL TOWN SOUTHERN ROMANCE

- *Once Upon A Coffee* (Avery and Dillon)
- *To Get Me To You* (Cam and Norah)
- *Know Me Well* (Liam and Riley)
- *Be Careful, It's My Heart* (Brody and Tyler)
- *Just For This Moment* (Myles and Piper)
- *Wish I Might* (Reed and Cecily)
- *Turn My World Around* (Tucker and Corinne)
- *Dance Me A Dream* (Jace and Tara)
- *See You Again* (Trey and Sandy)
- *The Christmas Fountain* (Chad and Mary Alice)
- *You Were Meant For Me* (Mitch and Tess)
- *A Lot Like Christmas* (Ryan and Hannah)
- *Dancing Away With My Heart* (Zach and Lexi)

WISHING FOR A HERO SERIES (A WISHFUL SPINOFF SERIES)
SMALL TOWN ROMANTIC SUSPENSE

- *Make You Feel My Love* (Judd and Autumn)
- *Watch Over Me* (Nash and Rowan)
- *Can't Take My Eyes Off You* (Ethan and Miranda)
- *Burn For You* (Sean and Delaney)

MEET CUTE ROMANCE
SMALL TOWN SHORT ROMANCE

- *Once Upon A Snow Day*
- *Once Upon A New Year's Eve*
- *Once Upon An Heirloom*
- *Once Upon A Coffee*
- *Once Upon A Campfire*
- *Once Upon A Rescue*

SUMMER CAMP
CONTEMPORARY ROMANCE

- *Once Upon A Campfire*
- *Second Chance Summer*

Kait is a Mississippi native, who often swears like a sailor, calls everyone sugar, honey, or dar-lin', and can wield a bless your heart like a saber or a Snuggie, depending on requirements.

You can find more information on this

RITA ® Award-winning author and her books on her website http://kaitnolan.com. While you're there, sign up for her newsletter so you don't miss out on news about new releases!